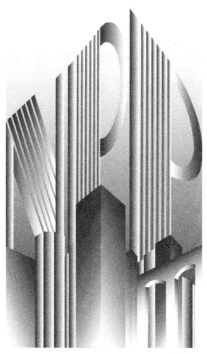

NU-PIKE PRESS

THE COFFEE MAKER

BY JAMES T.

THE COFFEE MAKER
Copyright 2024 by Jack Grisham

For information address:
Nu-Pike Press, P.O. Box 735
Huntington Beach, California 92648
nupikepress@gmail.com

Edited by
Rachel Goldin

Cover Art
Julia Kwong

Hand on the Pump lyrics © BMG Rights Management, Soul Assassins Inc, Universal Music Publishing Group used by acknowledgement.

Lyrics from "Gee, Officer Krupke" used by acknowledgement. Songwriters: Stephen Sondheim / Leonard Bernstein / Arthur Laurents.

"Men die outside the door, as starving beggars die on cold nights in cruel cities in the dead of winter. Die for want of what is within their grasp. They live on the other side of it— live because they have not found it. Nothing else matters compared to helping them find it, and open it, and walk in, and find Him. So, I stand by the door."

— Rev. Sam Shoemaker

A SERIES OF SURRENDERS

HALE FELLOWS, WELL MET

"You can't get a decent meal around here. Yeah, we've got that fusion joint on Atlantic, but I'll tell you Jamie, that hostess can be a real bitch."

"Come on, sweetheart. Why don't we back it down a bit?"

"'We?' Who's 'we' Bob? What are you saying?" She turned back to Jamie, the dark cuff of her jacket swimming through her scampi in white sauce. "He thinks she's cute. What is she, a little high-school tramp, and you got the hots for her? You're fucking disgusting."

The table for four had become the centerpiece of Antonio's on 8th. Connie's seemingly bottomless glass of Merlot had set the stage.

"I'm not speaking of the hostess, Connie. You're getting loud."

"I'm loud? Your *fucking* tie is loud— anyway, Jamie sweetie, I bet that little bitch—"

"Excuse me, ma'am… "

Connie turned coldly disturbed toward the maître d'.

"I was wondering if you might employ a gentler tone."

She held her frosted countenance in place as she reached for the bottle and purposely over-poured her glass— the deep red rosé offending the tablecloth. "—And I was wondering if you could bring us another bottle of this fucking salad dressing?"

She laughed as she shook the empty.

"I'm afraid the kitchen is a bit busy at the moment."

Robert put a well-rehearsed touch on Connie's arm. "—Connie, please."

"Don't fucking 'Connie' me. Why the fuck are those pricks getting served? I don't see him cutting them off."

She slid her chair back and rose to her feet. Staggering, she snatched a bottle of chilled champagne from the table to their right. "—Sorry kids, kitchen's closed." She upended the bottle and swallowed hard— a bubbling mouthful cascading down her blouse.

Jamie donned his sweater.

"Where are you going? I haven't seen you in years and now you've gotta go?" She inhaled another slug of champagne. "Seriously, sugar, sit down, stop being a bitch." She turned on Robert. "—look what you're doing, driving away our friends. Is this ever gonna stop?"

He took a deep breath and withheld his anger. "You're the problem here, Connie. Not me."

"That's right. I'm the problem, and you're the cunt— how's that?"

A waiter grabbed the borrowed bottle from her hand. "—We've called the police."

"Good, let em come—" She threw a handful of scampi across the room. "—you murdered the fucking shrimp. Murderers!"

Robert grabbed her around the waist. She threw her head back and broke his nose— the warm blood flowing through cuckold-fingers. She stepped forward and landed a pro-boxing punch on the maître d's chin.

"Take that, you fucking cocksucker."

The police entered the restaurant.

Connie stood opposed— a suburban dipsomaniac gunslinger with an arsenal of Gwyneth Paltrow memes and a Louis Vuitton handbag.

"Are you fucking kidding me… *the police*?" She shoved the injured Robert aside and stepped forward. "—watch yourself patrons, it's the fucking restaurant patrol looking for free meals and law-breaking dinner rolls. Hide your dirty napkins, diners. The fuzz is here!"

"Could you please step outside, ma'am?"

"Sidestep? You want me to sidestep? How's this?" She swagged and shuffled as she tripped over a chair and slammed into a table.

"Ma'am, I've instructed you to step outside." The officer unholstered his taser as she approached.

"Are you even legal? Let's see a green card, you fucking border nigg— Arghhh!"

The taser banged steady— a bullseye pop to Connie's midsection that left the racial slur hanging in midair as her body convulsed electrified to the ground.

*****

Albert checked his left as he pulled into traffic. The '78 Monte Carlo slow crept down the boulevard.

"I hope that fucking *puto* Tony comes creeping around."

"Jesus Beto— let it go, eh?"

"What do you fucking care what I say about him? You want something there?"

"I don't give a fuck about that old prick. I was just little."

"Yeah and he's rolling six-zero— fucking *chomo*, man."

The city center was backlit as the sun slid behind the twin towers. The river reflected the lights from above— the streets of the *barrio*.

"Look Tina, I don't give a fuck who you used to be."

"Why should you?"

"I don't— I told you, as long as you don't bring then into now."

He pulled to the sidewalk. The Monte's wheels brushed smooth against the red corner curb of Caesar's Blue Fairy Liquor.

He opened the door.

Tina followed in kind.

"Where the fuck you going, huh?"

"I wanna get something too."

"I'll get it for you."

"No way Beto. I'm not drinking that weak-ass shit."

Albert pulled his door closed. Tina slid back into her seat.

"You're not getting fucked up at *mi hermano's*. My Nina doesn't need some sloppy bitch cruising her birthday."

"Fuck you, Beto. I had to drag your fucking ass out of the fucking street last week. You were so fucked up you couldn't even walk. Don't fucking tell me."

He came up hard, twisted over the center console and, with his knee, pinned her against the torn gold tuck and roll. He slammed the back of her head against factory glass. "—you should shut your fucking mouth before you get something stuffed in it."

She struggled to breathe as he held her. The neon liquor store sign reflected two-dollar ninety-nine madness in his eyes.

"You got something you want to say now?"

He released her throat but stayed heavy upon her.

"No, baby."

"Yeah… no baby. Should've fucking 'no-baby'd' before I split your fucking lip."

He released her and left the car.

"Beto!"

"Hey Nina."

He kissed the young girl on her cheek. His heavy malt breath clung to her skin. He pulled two crumpled twenties and a ten from his pocket, pushed them into her hand. "—there's no card, baby, but if you want you could get yourself one."

"Thanks, *tío*." She wiped her face. "—love you."

"Ah, you too, *Chica*." The young girl ran toward her friends. He called to her. "—*Mi hermano*?"

"—He's dancing!"

Albert pulled an open 40 from a brown paper bag. He was thirty-six minutes from the liquor store and two 40s deep. He one-gulped the third to the midway as he staggered onto the dancefloor. Eyes closed, he fell in step with the song. *"Hand on the pump, left hand on a forty…"*

The gun tucked behind his waistband was blue-metal flash. Low cool, elbows up, side to side, he grooved. Step left, step right.

"Yo Beto!"

"*Oralé* Eddie!"

"Nina, your *tío* is fucked up, eh?"

The two girls laughed as Albert stumbled.

"Yeah, my *Papi* told him not to come like loaded, but I guess he didn't hear him, huh? Fucking *bien pedo!*"

The hanging lights strung in the trees sent shards of angel cool across Tina's face. She danced without care— a late summer promise wrapped in a used floral dress. Carelessly she twirled, stumbling into an old friend. His eyes scanned the yard as he stepped toward her and pulled her close. His hands walked down her hips as she swayed.

"*Hola, Chava.*"

She ignored his greeting but pushed against him. The crowd on the dance floor concealed his touch.

Albert, oblivious, pulled the gun from his waistband as a new groove stepped hard. The pistol hung heavy in his hand. The arms of the alcohol cradled him as the voice of its effect softly whispered. "—Beto… Beto, *te quiero.*"

Tina dropped to her knees and pulled the man's waist against her. He put his hands in her hair, pushing her face against the lines of his now stiffening cock— her bare knees, tearing on rough patio pavers.

Albert wavered in the corner, his gun searching out the stars, as he floated in and out of consciousness.

"Eddie, fucking Beto is here."

"I know. I saw him."

"He's got that fucking *puta* with him— fucking Tina."

"*Es nada*, I talked to him."

"What'd you tell him?"

"I told him he'll be cool for Nina."

"Cool for Nina? *Ay Cabrón!* He's pissing on Nina's bike and his fucking crazy bitch is sucking Tony's cock."

Albert hoisted his pants and slid back to the groove. Eddie grabbed him by the bare skin of his neck— a young pup held in place.

"Beto, what the fuck, man? You're fucking up, dude. Blanca says you gotta go."

"Blanca? I just got here, eh?"

"Yeah, your fucking woman just got here too." Eddie turned his brother to face Tina. Her ass against Tony— grinding as his hands fluttered unhindered beneath her dress.

Albert stumbled toward her as he came into the moment. He grabbed her arm, twisting it behind her back. "—I fucking told you, bitch."

"I was dancing… I didn't do nothing—"

Albert looked into Tony's eyes and smiled. "—*Oralé chomo*."

*****

Lee's Liquor Mart was on the hill above Highway 19. Mr. Lee was a purveyor of bottom shelf liquors and the coldest beer in town.

I often stop at Lee's— shit, that sounds a tink too formal for this kind of thing. I'm supposed to be giving you my thoughts, not testifying in court. Often, is misleading, your honor. I was in rehab earlier this year, jumped on psych meds for a week or two, attempted a marijuana maintenance program, and then I just plain old white-knuckled it until

I just couldn't fucking stand it anymore and now, here I am, strutting towards that one-hundred-proof oasis on the hill with the cocksure bounce of a boy who knows what it's gonna take to put things right— say 'Hallelujah!'

"Hey Jacob, where you been?"

"What's happening, Grady? Where's Mr. Lee?"

"Vacation— extended with pay."

Grady had more fingers than teeth, more wants than sense. He was from somewhere down South, but how he got out here and working in a convenience store I got no idea.

Jacob pulled open a double glass door— the cold brews huddling behind frosted panes. He held up a 16-ounce can of Pabst. "—don't you guys got sixers of this shit?"

"Yeah, look down. Lee keeps it on the bottom shelf— colder than a witches' titty-tit."

Jacob bent down and grabbed the beers— laughed on his way up. "—Shit, Grady this feels more like a nun's pussy than a witches' nipple. It's fucking frozen. You gotta tell Lee to turn that shit down."

"Ha! God-damn-it, Jacob. Quit your crying."

The cash register was giving Grady trouble. He'd been there close to a year and it was still a mystery.

"Why you white boys drink that shit, anyway?"

"It's the mighty blue ribbon, the PBR— check me, I'm a rocker through and through."

"Rocker my ass— fucking punk, I thought you worked at that car place."

"Not in my heart, I don't." Jacob set the ice-cold sixer on the counter. He smiled as he unfolded a twenty and dropped it in Grady's hand.

"How's that little girl of yours?"

"Always here—" Jacob tapped his heart. "I'll tell her you asked about her. She'll love it."

Grady pulled a lemon-raspberry sucker from a plastic display case. "You tell her it's from me now."

"Yeah, you and Mr. Lee."

There was a relaxed groove to his step as he strolled back to his truck. He didn't know what it was, but just buying the booze made him feel better— instant relief.

That's the problem with this shit. A couple of cold brews get the blame for all sorts of misfortune when, in reality, it's bad luck that should take the blame, and the brews should get the credit for making the intolerable tolerable.

He laughed as he rolled down the window, sat back in his seat, and pulled the tab on a whole lot of feel-better.

I know bosses are supposed to make things difficult but Mr. Grant's a fucking master of putting screws to my balls. I can't work any harder, and I can't get out in front of my bills— what the fuck does he want from me?

He watched a grey moth bounce against the front glass— seeking exit to the world. One, two, three times it tried— pounding its head against the window frame, and then it gave up. It landed on its back on the dashboard and stayed put.

And then there's court— Jesus. I understand them taking a swipe at my finances for that last driving-impaired charge but enough is enough. I learned my fucking lesson, man. They need to back the fuck off. How the fuck am I supposed to get on the straight and narrow when they got their fingers so far up my ass? You know what I need, I need a couple months of clear water to get my stroke going— shit, that beer is cold!

He put a tombstone on the first tall boy, threw the empty out the window, and popped the top on another.

Krys can be rough, man. She can't expect me to work all day and then come home without taking a break in between. It's too much. I love her and C.C., but sometimes I just need a minute for myself— a little spot of my own, even if it's only a couple of bucket seats and a bench in the back where I can stretch the fuck out and let that workday poison seep out of me— it's not even a want, it's a fucking necessity, man.

Another empty set sail out the window and landed somewhere nearby— hopefully the bed of the truck, but he wasn't sure— nor did he care as he popped the top on another.

She thinks I'm bad. I ain't bad— not even close. I know guys that can't stand their kids; they cheat on their wives— total fucking assholes walking around like fat swinging dicks on parade. Krys gets mad at me when I'm an hour or two late. I know guys that don't even bother coming home— what do they say? 'Fuck 'em if they can't take a joke.'

He took a drink, rested the can against his lips and inhaled the alcoholic perfume of promise and weekends spent in the yard laughing and cutting it up with his friends— good times... unbothered times.

Maybe those guys got it right. Stay gone until they miss you and then blow back into town like a fucking superstar— Daddy's home, baby!

The scent of night jasmine crawled over the burnt cigarette butts in the ashtray as the diesel fumes from the big rigs on the highway hovered above. The moth hadn't moved. He touched it with his finger— no response. He threw an empty out the window and popped the top on another.

You know, my father was a drunk— mom was too, or maybe her drunk was just a drunk to keep his drunk from hurting so much. Either way, they say this uh, alcoholic personality is a family thing, and if I do have it— which seems pretty fucking ridiculous, then it's nothing I should be blamed for. It's in my blood— pre-mixed.

He threw an empty out the window and popped the top on another.

It was getting dark.

He checked his watch— 8:30.

Krys is gonna be pissed when I get home.

"Jacob, you still alive?" Grady was leaning against the outside of his truck— black hands wide on the window frame. Jacob could smell his breath— menthol cigarettes, malt liquor: stale grocery clerk air.

"Hey bro, I said you alright, man?"

"Yeah, what's up?"

"You are, fucker. You gonna pick up these cans?"

"I'm tossing 'em in the back."

Grady stomped on one of the tall boys lying at his feet. "—You ain't making it."

Jacob stuck his head out the window and looked down— five dead soldiers looking back at him. "—I gotta get the fuck out of here, dude."

"You ain't gonna nowhere like that. Here— let me do you something. Hold out that hand."

Grady tapped out a nice fat line of white powder on the top of Jacob's fist— the blueish white crystals picking up the last light of day.

Jacob leaned over, held the right side of his nose closed and he inhaled hard. The cool inner-city-white burned but not unpleasantly so.

"Oh-fuck-man, that's uh…" his head was trying to step into reality but it was still running loose in the weeds. "Let me get one more, buddy— just a little bit. Touch me up."

Grady did him right.

He thanked the clerk for his kindness and, as he was pulling away, he tossed the last empty out the window. He fishtailed out of the parking lot. Three miles. He could make it. No problem…

JAMES

It was a 1976 Eldorado convertible— Rio red. The beast was shit on mileage but he loved the way it would float across the lanes and with the top down and the heater on during a cold night drive it was made for adventure. He was parked along the drainage ditch— the coffee wasn't cutting it, and the desert sun had turned his styling gel to liquid. He could feel it dripping like crude oil down the back of his neck. He called his wife as he brushed another lazy fly off his cheek.

"Hey baby, what's up?"

"I thought you were giving a talk. Where are you?"

"Arlo— fly capital of the United States."

"Where the hell is Arlo?"

"Do you remember when we drove out to Lone Ridge— stopped at that little place past Chester?"

"The vintage shop?"

"Yeah— you got that fucking rabbit skull or whatever the fuck it was."

"Coyote."

"Well, that's where I am— the middle of fucking nowhere. I bet if I held the phone out you could hear me dying."

She gave him a moment of silence. "—Nope, I don't hear anything but drama. Are there drunks in Arlo?"

"Yeah, there's four of us— the secretary, the treasurer, some maniac going on about some sort of alien intervention, and me— why the fuck do I keep doing this shit?"

"Because you don't say no."

Their club was in a storefront. The window said Billiards, but from the look of it there hadn't been a table there in years. There were two rusted ceiling fans spinning, one, slowly to the right, and one, sort of skipping off cockeyed to the left. There was dirt on the floor— linoleum beneath it, but if that tile had seen a mop, it was during the cowboy days.

"James?"

The man was weathered— a worn desert-brown face shimmering over a faded blue-jean shirt and pants.

What'd my kid call that look, a Canadian Tuxedo? That's right.

James laughed as he stuck out his hand. If the old rustler was offended, he didn't show it— *he's probably used to people walking around laughing to themselves.* "How you doing, old-timer?"

"We're doing it one day at a time, James."

Jesus— we gotta get some new cliches. I swear to God, you could have a whole conversation with some of these sober cats, and say nothing but the slogans— One Day at a Time, Live and Let Live, and all that other crap— they'd think you were really connecting.

"That's right, pops, taking it like it comes, brother— God's will and all that."

The old man was pleased.

A twice-beaten four-door sedan led a cloud of high desert dust into the parking lot.

"You expecting a good turnout?"

"We should have about twenty. That new rehab said they were gonna bring the van— a bunch of hungry alcoholic souls to feed."

"Excellent. I don't like giving my pitch on humility unless it's a full house."

The meeting started on time. Sixteen recovering alcoholics—including James, hunkered down out of the unforgiving gaze of the desert sun. It reminded him of those old Jewish mystics running around in the Sinai seeing visions and creating gods. He stood dressed in a black suit and a white t-shirt behind a lectern at the front of the room. There was a small 'Easy Does It' sticker hanging without hope on the splintered wood.

"How you folks doing? I'm James T. and I am an alcoholic."

"Hey James!"

"And I love being sober and I love being here and I wanna thank myself for coming out."

They weren't too sure of what to make of that last bit— thanking myself. Trained to thank God for everything— as far as they figured, they had nothing to do with being sober. God got 'em there, kept 'em there and did all the work. I wonder why he got 'em loaded?

"Sobriety starts with a room. For some of us, it might be a hospital or a well-appointed rehab, for others a church basement or the comfort of your own home… for some of us, sobriety begins in jail.

"I got sober when I was twenty-six years old. I was a failed rocker who lived with his mother. I was married to one woman and having a child with another. I couldn't hold a job. I could *get* one— I just couldn't hold one. I wasn't a big fan of being told what to do… or keeping my hands to myself. It seemed like the world was against me. No matter how hard I tried, I failed, and in the morning, I'd wake to find terror, frustration, bewilderment, and despair hanging like death by my bedside. I was miserable. Jesus, some of these fuckers talk about alcohol being a problem, but I felt better when I was drinking. Shit… I liked you when I had one or two in me. Throw in a couple of pills, and I fucking loved you, man— I'd cuddle afterwards. And, if you were being extremely generous, and you frosted that sauce up with a line of cocaine,

I'd want to start a business with you."

He stared over the small crowd and smiled as if he was standing in the past and looking at something that only he could see. Their laughter brought him back to the room.

"But if you caught me sober and having one of my days, I was a stressed-out, fear-based, anxiety-ridden motherfucker who wanted you nothing more than dead— right now! Crazy thing is… I thought you were the problem. I was incapable of seeing the truth. How the fuck did I know I had a mental illness?"

He spoke to a woman in the second row as if they were the only ones there— one alcoholic talking to another.

"I took a look at that pamphlet they got— twenty questions, forty, sixty. I wasn't sure how many fucking questions they had, but it was a joke: was I blacking out? Yeah, so what? Missing work? As much as fucking possible. Hanging out with lower companions— look, it's not like I was in church and asking the guy next to me if he wanted to knock down a couple lines of blow and rob a liquor store after the sermon. I was surrounded by my equals, like pigs in a sty. They used like I used. They hurt like I hurt. Thank God, or whatever you wanna believe in— one day, one of those pigs— an alcoholic maniac that I called friend got himself arrested on a cocaine trafficking charge. He was a real mouthy little prick— wasn't cut out for jail— not like you sir…"

He smiled at the recently released convict in the front row— a man with the words 'mama's boy' tattooed over his left eye.

"If anyone was cut out for jail, it would definitely be you."

The small room filled with laughter— mama's boy grinning like a mid-November Jack-o-lantern in a Halloween parade.

"But as I was saying, in exchange for a cell, this jail-terrified buddy of mine copped a plea. He said he had a problem and they sent him off to rehab. When he got out— all spic and span, shiny and new, he brought me a twelve-step message of recovery— like I'm doing for you today, and for some reason I bought it. I fell in love with this deal. I was in."

I can always tell when the room is with me— when the doubt and mistrust slip away and they realize I'm one of their own. I want them to see me and think that if I can do it— this whacked-out old rocker, that they can too.

"I once heard somebody say that it's hard to do something good for yourself when you're so full of self-hate. I get it, man— why do you think I thank myself for coming out? I've been here before and I didn't do a fucking thing to stay, and I'll lay good money that I'm not the only repeat offender in this room… "

He let that sink in.

They didn't have to tell me. I knew what they had going on. It's a rare thing when an alcoholic or an addict shows up in the rooms without ever trying to quit before— this is a program of people who couldn't stay stopped.

"For most of you, waking up is gonna be a real bitch. When you come face-to-face with the crap you've been pulling, the pain you've inflicted, the hell you've envisioned, when you *can't* imagine living *with or without alcohol*, then you're probably one step away from punching your own ticket. The old-timers call that the 'jumping-off point.' I've been there, man. I've had the rope in my hand. But if you're new, and you can hear what I'm saying, I beg you to just hang tough for one day— one fucking dust-filled desert day is all its gonna take to get this thing rolling. You can do it, baby. I believe in you."

He took a drink of water and thought back to when he used to gulp down abandoned drinks on restaurant tables.

"I'm fifty-six years old. My sobriety began thirty years ago in a room just like this. Shit, we had the same fucking linoleum tile on our floor— albeit not as dirty as this one, but it was dirty. It might have been white at one time, but the coffee stains and years of stumbling-drunk traffic had turned it a deathly grey. We had a couple of couches— big nasty looking things, but I never sat on 'em for fear of crabs. And there were slogans on the walls— you know 'em, say 'em with me: 'One Day at a Time,' 'Easy Does It,' 'Live and Let Live.'" He glanced at his watch. It was 7:30, no souls were saved after an hour. "—Jesus, I gotta wrap this up."

The small crowd, almost in unison, checked their time. He smiled.

They didn't realize how long we've been here— that's a good sign. Sometimes I see people checking their watches during my talk and it freaks me the fuck out. I get to thinking that I'm boring them, and then I get all wrapped up in my head.

"They say in recovery that there's a bolt for every nut and I believe that to be true. Alcoholism and drug addiction are equal opportunity employers— you might even call this America's true melting pot. We band together because we know that without each other we will surely die— a common bond regardless of race, creed, sex, religious preferences, or color. We leave our differences at the door. And don't you worry about losing yourself in here— no matter what you may have seen or heard, we're not looking for robots— mindless drones quoting tired antiquated phrases. We want you to be you. We've already got a me. Join us."

They circled up and held hands. He didn't normally join the prayer circle at home— not because he was against it, he just didn't feel it like they did. His relationship with whatever power there might be, was more on a personal level. He didn't bother God, and God didn't bother him.

He shook a few hands, gave his number to a few people that would almost certainly never call, and he thanked his host for the opportunity to be of service. It was a three-hour drive home. He had plenty of time in the car to kick his own ass. It might not have been his favorite pastime, but it was the one he indulged in the most.

LEGAL TROUBLE

His lawyer's office was a shrine to Little League baseball and teen service projects. It was in a strip mall— Suite F, above the shoe repair and the Chinese laundry. The laundry specialized in one-day service. His lawyer specialized in youth sports and bad news.

"Jacob, there's nothing I can do about it. It's your third driving under the influence and they're going to want some jail time."

"But I wasn't driving. I was stopped."

His lawyer sighed and lit a cigarette. The ashtray was full of butts— drunk drivers, divorces, child support, simple assaults— all of 'em, smoked clean down to the filter. He opened Jacob's file— a yellow legal pad in a green stock binder. "—Are you fucking with me? You were stopped because you slammed into the back of a parked car. You're lucky it wasn't occupied, or we'd be having a whole different conversation."

Jacob had a black eye and a cut lip. When he smiled, the scab cracked. "I was trying to make light."

His lawyer took another hit— his ash, an inch or two long and refusing to fall. "—Maybe light isn't the thing we're looking for." He thumbed through the police report. "Did they do a blood test at the hospital? I'm not seeing the count."

"I didn't go to a hospital."

"I don't see a breath test here— how did they conclude you were inebriated?"

"I don't know."

"What do you mean you don't know? You were arrested for DUI."

"I don't remember."

"You don't remember being arrested?"

"No, I don't. I woke up in the morning— tried to get out of the backyard—"

"What… what the hell are you talking about?"

"I was *so* fucked up. I thought I was on a patio. I kept pulling on the back gate— trying to get out, but I was locked in a cell— I only had a couple of beers."

"You were compliant."

"I don't know."

"No, it says here you were compliant, but there's no statements admitting guilt?" He tossed the report on the desk. "—They found nothing in the truck— no bottles, paraphernalia, controlled substance?"

"Nothing— I was clean, man."

The lawyer, Rue Marshal, looked over his glasses at Jacob. His ash surrendered to the desktop— he blew it to the floor. "—You don't even remember getting arrested. How the hell would you know if you were clean?"

"I'd know if I had shit in my truck. I was clean, dude. I'd been doing good. I fucked up a couple weeks ago, but— what do you got? You got something, don't you? You're the fucking man, Rue. I knew you could help."

Marshal rolled a pen across his desk— stubby, nicotine-stained fingers, pushing the fine-tip Uni-Ball red.

"I might have something, but I almost wish I didn't. Look, it's not my job to tell you what you should and shouldn't be doing, but I'd feel better knowing that you weren't driving around under the influence while I'm out to dinner with my wife and kids."

"You can get me off."

"No, as much as I'd like to, I'm not going to *get you off*."

"Ugh, come on Rue, that's not what I meant."

"I know what you meant. Have you ever had a court card?"

"No."

"Not even on that last charge? I thought we set that up."

"Not me. I paid that fine— two fucking grand, and you signed me up for that fucking rehab thing."

"Oh, that's right— look how that worked out."

Rue tapped the last cigarette from his pack— crumpled the empty soft box as he contemplated his pitch. "We've got prelim on Monday. I think I can get this dropped, but you're gonna have to play ball."

"Fuck, I'll do whatever you want— just keep me out of jail."

Rue paused for a moment... *here it is, my chance to bring out that Tommy Lasorda shit— motivation and enlightenment bestowed upon a young man worthy of a good life.* He took another drag and stepped onto the mound. "You know, Jacob, sometimes people think they're getting a break but in reality, they'd be doing better if there was a price to pay."

"Pro bono?"

"God-damn-it. You know that's not what I'm talking about— get the fuck out of here."

Jacob twice knuckled the desk, stood, and turned for the door.

"Hey kid—"

The smile on Jacob's face as he looked back was wider than the gap between. "Yeah?"

"Wear a suit."

"You got it, Skipper."

There was a light rain falling as Krystal and C.C. drove Jacob to a twelve-step meeting— four miles down and not a word yet spoken.

I can't look at him. Sure, C.C. is fine in the back with her game—

she loves her dad, but the sound of Jacob breathing next to me is making me sick. I should've packed up and split after that first arrest— writing on the wall and all that bullshit. This is exactly what my dad did to my mom— she was a dishrag. My father promised nothing— it was one big letdown, no hope on the horizon. He gave it to us as if we had it coming. Is that what my baby deserves— a daddy like that, a fucking asshole exhaling disappointment with every breath? I'm not buying this shit anymore. That 'stand by your man' crap is a fucking joke.

"I'm so fucking over it, Jacob. You have no idea what you do to us. You're a fucking loser."

"Come on Krys, C.C."

"Don't fucking 'C.C.' me. You don't give a fuck about her."

"Stop it."

"Why don't *you* fucking stop it... or better yet, why don't you apologize again for missing her fucking birthday?"

"Dad?"

"Ceace, shut it."

"Don't talk to her like that."

"I don't think you've got any right to tell me how to talk to my daughter."

"Jesus, Krys, I don't know why you're so bent out of shape. I said I was sorry. Marshal got the charges dropped. I'm fixing the truck. I fucked up, baby— people make mistakes."

"A mistake? Is that what you're calling these now, mistakes?"

"You know, Rue plays ball with the judge— he's got juice downtown. Twenty-eight meetings— that's it, that's all I gotta do, and it's over."

"I don't give a fuck what that fucking pedophile did to get you off."

"He's a good guy—"

"He's a fucking creep."

Jacob stared out the window— a beaten dog watching the cars go by— *I fucked up, and this is the price you pay to be married. A couple days of getting my ass dragged through the mud, and then hopefully it gets better. I wish she wouldn't do it in front of C.C. though. It's not good for a little girl to see her dad getting yelled at.* "—When are you guys coming back?"

"It's a school night. Find your own ride."

"It's fucking raining, Krys. You took my phone."

"Shut up." She stopped in lanes, cars honking behind her. "Shut the fuck up and get out."

Jacob opened the door, but before exiting he reached for C.C. They touched hands. "—I love you, bug."

"You too, dad."

"Get out."

They were gone before he stepped on the curb.

THE HALL ON THE HILL

The hall was a 1940s women's club on the edge of Weatherly Park. A group of recovered drunks had purchased the land and the building from the city in the early seventies. There was a large parking lot at the front and a smaller lot out back. This is where Jacob stood in his red jacket and his blue jeans and his wet shoes that had gotten that way from walking up the grass hill from the street. He lit a cigarette and watched the crowd shuffle in.

These people don't look like drunks.

He recognized the cute checker from the market and the guy who ran the stationery shop on 17th.

I bought a fucking apology card for Krys, and that guy rang me up. It didn't do me any good. I found it in the trash unopened. I wonder if I know any more of these 'don't look like a drunk drunks?' I know lots of wet ones— they're fun as fuck, but these other ones, the dry ones that look like normal people, they could be trouble. It just ain't right. They should have to wear a letter or something— a big alcoholic 'A' on their shirts so you know what's coming. That'd fix 'em.

The rain had turned into a mist that haloed around the lights on the roof of the building. It would have been beautiful if he'd bothered to notice. There was a row of No Parking signs that'd been ignored— *I guess the rules don't apply to them either.*

He took a few more hits and then he walked toward the light from an open door in the back. It led to a small kitchen. He could see the crowd beyond— their laughter and their chatter seeping into the parking lot. He imagined a flock of cartoon birds cackling about whose booze was whose.

This court card thing is a real bitch— twenty-eight signatures in sixty days. What if I get sick? I got a fucking stomach-ache right now. Hey, maybe that chick from the market could sign a couple of lines— I see her giving me the occasional eyeball when I'm wandering through produce. I could cruise by there in the morning— chat her up. I bet she'd go for it. Fuck, they probably have some sort of registry or something.

He looked his card over. It didn't seem too complicated— no visible hidden codes.

"How you doing, bud?" The man walked by Jacob without waiting for an answer. He passed through the kitchen door and disappeared into the hall. Jacob tossed the short end of his smoke onto the gravel drive and followed.

There was a guy in the kitchen tinkering with a large empty coffee pot— fooling with its inner workings. He looked alright— another one of those 'not like a drunk drunks,' but Jacob could see the edges on this one. He looked to be in his mid-fifties, but his hair was long. It hung down to his shoulders, and he had the look of a model or one of those men in the magazines that Krys was always looking at— *maybe he was a hairdresser.* Jacob laughed.

"Hey, can you hang on to this?"

"Yeah, sure man—" Jacob grabbed the empty pot.

"I gotta refill that thing— fucking drunks and their coffee, man. Hey, do me a favor, dude— take that out back and piss in it."

He had to be joking, but he dead-stared into Jacob's eyes— *this guy is a fucking lunatic.* The man laughed as he took the pot back. "I'm just fucking with you, kid— you new?"

"Yeah, I guess."

An elderly man walked into the kitchen. "—He doesn't look new. He looks used."

The coffee guy threw a wet sponge at him. "—Get the fuck out of here, Pops." He turned back to Jacob. "Don't trip on him, kid— fucking wet brain. That's what happens when you don't stop in time." He held out his hand. "—I'm James. Nice to meet you."

"Jacob."

James turned a faucet on and let the water flow— he tested the heat with his hand. The hot steam rising over his fingers.

A wave of laughter washed in from the hall.

"Oh man, you gotta check this dude out, kid. He's fucking solid." James put a wet hand on Jacob's shoulder. He steered him toward the door to the main room. "You'll love this guy."

There was a flamboyantly-dressed man standing behind a lectern at the front of the room. He was wearing a dark blue suit with an orange ascot.

Shit, this old dude is pushing ninety— maybe a hundred, but he's got that fruity old Mr. Adams vibe— my twelfth-grade art teacher— nice hair though, looks like a bob-cut Jesus without the beard.

The place was packed— every seat filled. There was a strange energy in the air— a buzz that was startling in its intensity. The crowd was pumped. The old man was on one.

"Don't be so arrogant that you think you can just walk in here and get sober." He let his gaze travel the room; when he lit upon Jacob he winked. "—You're dealing with a mental illness, be it Park Place or park bench, Yale or jail, you can't just tap out when you feel like it."

You know, I can't say I was stoked to be here, but this is kinda cool. Fucking guy is like an actor or something— up there on the stage, prancing around, laying it out— Romeo, hey, Romeo, show me your dick. Ha! A fucking gay soap opera.

"Now I don't know about you, but I couldn't see the truth, even if it was laid right in front of me. I'm not an alcoholic— those cops are pricks."

The room filled with laughter. Jacob felt as if the old man was speaking to him, but he was sure he wasn't— the wink was accidental. The distance, too great.

"It's like my friend Ricky there—" the old guy gestured to a large man in the front row. "—He can't see the truth either. He's not fat. His pants are tight."

The laughter soared— Ricky howling as loud as the rest.

"I hate to break it to you buddy, but that's a stretch waistband."

Jacob caught himself drawn into the spirit of the crowd. He loved shit talking— chopping it up with the guys at work. *This old fruit is taking the granny out of his buddy. It's fucking awesome.*

The audience broke into applause. Jacob followed suit.

James appeared at his shoulder. "—It's easier to swallow the truth with a bit of laughter. You didn't laugh, did you? You know we got you if you laugh."

"No—" Jacob reinstated his guard. "—he was funny, but I was back here, so it was kinda hard to hear, you know."

"Yeah, I know."

The crowd got to their feet. They made a large prayer circle as James went back to the coffee room. A woman grabbed Jacob's right hand— a young girl his left.

"God—" Jacob didn't know the prayer, so he mouthed the words. "—grant me the serenity to accept the things I cannot change, the courage to change the things I can, and the wisdom to know the difference."

When they released hands, he followed James.

"Here you go man—" the coffee maker handed him a towel. "—why don't you stick around and help me clean up."

"I've gotta get my card signed."

"Start drying— I'll handle the card."

Jacob was grateful to be out of the main room. They seemed as if they were all friends— hugging and fawning over each other.

As they dried the pots and wiped the counters, various people stopped by to say hello to James.

I guess I hooked up with the right guy. You wouldn't expect the coffee maker to have the juice, but these drunks are a strange breed. I'm gonna get my card signed without having to stand in line or whatever they do here— maybe James will toss me a few extra signatures for helping out.

"I liked that guy—" Jacob hung up his towel. "—he reminded me of old Mr. Adams— the cock-goblin of Pacific View High."

"Mr. Adams, eh? I didn't know you rolled like that— sorry Jacob, Alan's straight. He's been married for like fifty years."

"I'm not gay."

"You're not?"

"No, I've got a wife."

"Oh, you're one of those secretive weenie-lickers."

"Are you fucking with me?"

"Are you being judgmental and paranoid? Clothes don't make the man— or the woman."

"I'm sorry, I was just—"

"I know what you were doing, and I *was* fucking with you, but around here we're family and careful of how we talk about people— especially when they're not here to defend themselves."

"I wasn't attacking him— I thought he was cool. I don't give a fuck what he does."

"There you go, 'Live and Let Live.' You'll hear that a lot around here." James wiped his hands and put on a black leather coat. "—And, if you were a weenie-licker, or any other kinda liquor, we wouldn't give a fuck. It's none of our business. I looked like a maniac when I rolled in— blue hair, wearing my pajamas in the meetings— morning or night, and I never got anything but love and acceptance from that old man. He always had a kind word. I've heard some of these short-timers talking about old program and how hard they were, but I've been sober thirty years and I never saw it. The day I came in, that old guy told me I had two million people rooting for me— two million. A world-wide community of clean and sober people wanting nothing but for me to succeed."

He pulled his keys out of his pocket— a small brass medallion hanging on the ring.

"You got those people too… if you want 'em."

Jacob wasn't sure if he was expecting a reply. He checked his watch. " —Do you think one of those two million would give me a ride home?"

"Ha— you little prick. I got you. I'll even throw in a slice of pie."

THE DINER

Jacob had been there before— the diner on Aurora Ave North— Cindy's Pancake Palace. They served more than breakfast— at least, that's what the sign said, but Jacob had never been there in the evening. The crowd was different after dark. There was a table of high school kids getting loud in the corner and a man sitting solitary at the bar.

That dude looks homeless, but maybe he's not. James has me all screwed up on that judgement thing. Fuck— how are you supposed to just look at people as people? You know what that comes from? It's those drunks that don't look like drunks, so nobody looks like anything. That's no way to live man. You gotta be able to sum up the talent.

Jacob recognized Ricky— the heavyset guy, and Alan, who was talking to some young punk in the hallway. There was also a bunch of other people that he'd seen at the hall— nobody special.

I'd rather be home. This place rules in the morning— C.C. gets her happy face pancake, and I like that Big Breakfast, but God, I feel like a fucking hostage. I hope this doesn't take forever, but I can't see it going quick. James has something to say to everybody— he's one of those chatty chats, and he knows the whole fucking room. At least we didn't have to wait for a table.

"You guys want something to drink?"

James picked up a menu.

Come on dude, don't fucking order anything, don't order…

"Yeah, how about a couple of coffees." He looked to Jacob, "You cool with black?"

"Cream please… and sugar, lots of it."

"Thanks, Linda." James put the menu in the small metal rack on the table—*thank God.* "So, what's up?"

"With what?"

"With you. What are you doing here?"

This guy's gotta fucking screw loose. "—You're giving me a ride home. You wanted to stop by the diner."

"Jesus Christ. I know that. I'm not a fucking idiot. I meant, what are you doing *here*, why were you at the meeting— now sitting with me at the pancake palace. What's going on with your life, man?"

"Oh, I had to get my card signed, did you get it?" James pulled Jacob's card out of his jacket pocket and handed it to him. There was one signature and the date. "I was thinking you might've given me a couple extras for the coffee help."

James stared into Jacob's eyes— unflinching. "That's illegal."

"Oh, I didn't mean anything I just—"

"God, you're fucking easy, kid. Next time, sign it yourself. We're not connected with the courts. We do it as a favor, but that card is between you and them. There's nobody over at the club keeping tally of who comes in. You aren't the only cocksucker who snuck through that back door tonight— but if I was you, I'd do it the right way— get accountable to something, even if it's only a piece of paper and a couple of signatures."

The waitress sat the coffees down and walked off.

Jacob grabbed a handful of sugar packets, ripped the tops off and one by one dumped them in his coffee. He was five deep and pouring.

"You sure you're not here for a sugar issue?"

"No." He poured in two more as James watched the beverage

thicken up. "—I need to stop drinking."

"Do you think you have a problem?"

"Yeah, you signed my card— you know I do."

"That's not a drinking problem, kid— that's an appease the court problem. I'm asking *you if you think you* have a drinking problem."

"Yeah, I crashed my car."

"Circumstance— that's a busted car issue."

"My wife's on a fucking rampage."

"Circumstance— relationship issue. People get mad all the time and you being, or not being, an alcoholic doesn't have much to do with it."

"I'm on a fucking court-card— what do you want from me dude?"

"I'm asking *if you think you've* got a drinking problem."

"Well maybe you better tell me the answer you're looking for because I've got no idea what the fuck you're talking about."

"I'll make it simple.'

"Thank you."

"Have you honestly tried to quit before and if so, could you stay quit? Also, when you are drinking, how's the control thing working out for you?"

"Oh." Jacob looked around the room. Nobody, including the waitress, was concerned about the volume of their conversation.

I bet this fucker does this all the time— sitting on high, talking this shit; sipping his coffee like he doesn't have a care in the world.

"Have I honestly quit? I don't know. I think I have, but I never really thought about it before." He added another sugar. "As for the control thing— I like getting fucked up." Jacob laughed, but if James thought it was funny he didn't show it. "—Sorry, I guess I never thought about controlling it either. I do know I need to stop drinking. I have to."

"You have to? I wish it was that easy— to just stop when you have to. Do you know how many cats have sat where you are— tears in their eyes, telling me with all their heart, that if they don't stay clean, they're gonna go back to jail or lose their job or not be able to see their kids—

you know what I tell 'em?"

"What?"

"I tell 'em fuck you and fuck your job and fuck your kids."

"Come on, dude."

"No, you come on. If you got what I got— alcoholism, you're dealing with a mental illness. You heard Alan tonight. You can't just tap out when you feel like it. We're fucked up individuals, man. We will sit here and tell someone with all our hearts that we need to stop drinking, and we'll mean it— one-hundred-fucking-percent, and then we'll turn right around and go get fucked up again. You see, you may be hurting right now, and you might think that that court card and your pissed-off wife and your wrecked car and a coffee with me is gonna remind you that you don't ever wanna do this again, but you see, it's almost impossible for guys like you and I to remember the pain— to recall the hurt, the degradation, the remorse—if any, and after a while, we forget how we felt. We go about our lives thinking that we're normal men. And then one day you get thirsty, and that brain of yours tells you that you got this— you're good to go. That old drug and alcohol problem is nothing but dust in the rear-view mirror. And then you know what? That head of yours is gonna tell you that one drink won't hurt, and you'll take it— you'll drink again, and when you do, and that nightmare circus of pain and depravity creeps back into town, the best-case scenario— if you're lucky, if it doesn't kill you, you'll end up right back at this table, telling me that this time *you really mean it*."

"Do you want something, hun?" The waitress was standing behind Jacob, her hand on his shoulder. He felt like he was loaded— *who needs drugs when you got shit like this going on? This fucker is crazy.*

James tossed a sugar packet at him. "He wants a way out."

The waitress laughed. "Another forced dinner companion, James?"

"He's not forced, he's a volunteer. How about a couple slices of pie— whatever looks good. You cool with that, Jacob?"

"Yeah, but I gotta get going soon."

"Me too. Let me ask you something. Have you ever quit before? Have you ever woken up sick and said you weren't gonna do it again? Have you ever gone to jail, or rolled on some crazy fuck up, where you come to in the morning and swear off? Have you ever said that it's the booze that's doing it, so I'm just gonna smoke a little weed and keep it cool?"

"Ha! I went to some trippy rehab last year— wasn't like a twelve-step thing or anything, it was a— fuck. I can't even remember what we were doing, but it didn't work. I was clean for a couple of weeks— did their follow up and all that, but then I stopped by a friend's house and took a few bong hits. It wasn't long before I was drinking again— getting fucked up at work. I came in hammered and told my boss to fuck off."

James laughed at the similarity. "—Shit! How 'bout a raise, motherfucker! You're an animal, kid!"

Jacob sat back in his chair— fixed his collar. His red jacket and slicked back blond hair gave him a real James Dean vibe— *This guy ain't so bad. Maybe I was being too harsh on him.*

"You got a wife, Jacob— kids?"

"I been married six years. We got a little girl— C.C., she's eight."

"How's that, huh? What do they think?"

"My wife's pissed— fucking railed me on the way over, but Ceace loves me."

"Yeah, my kid loved me too, but it wasn't enough." James checked his watch. "—Let's get it to go, yeah?"

Jacob lived in a middle-class suburban neighborhood. The house was a well-kept mid-century modern— pink stucco, white trim.

We bought this place from Krys's mother. She gave us a good deal on the house— low down, low payments, and C.C.'s school is close. We used to live downtown— close to the bars and the action, but then, you got all that other craziness that comes with it. It's no place for a kid.

James stopped out front— the lawn was manicured, the bushes trimmed. He left the motor running. "You wanna check in with me?"

"Like a sponsor or something?" Jacob opened the door.

James shut off the engine. "I was thinking more like a friend. Most people don't have trouble calling friends. You put me on some level above you— this boss, or daddy role, and if you fuck up, well, it makes it harder for you to be honest. I don't want to be lied to, and if you do get in trouble, I want you to feel comfortable reaching out."

"I like that." Jacob put a foot on the curb. "—Okay then, I'll see you around."

James didn't move. "You may not know it, but you're fucking fragile, man. You just took a real ass-beating and who knows which way you're gonna go. That meeting hall may be the last house on the block for you— a quick stop before death, or it may be the first light out of the wilderness, like it was for me. You see, Jacob, it's not an issue of you stopping drinking, you're stopped right now. The issue is, you staying stopped."

James pulled a black business card from his jacket pocket— a white numeral 12 in large numbers embossed upon it. He handed it to Jacob. "I'm here to help if you want it, but I can't shove it down your throat. You gotta come get it."

You been shoving it for the last two hours— "Can I go now?"

"Yeah, you can go."

James was still sitting at the curb when Jacob walked through the front door —*what does he think I'm gonna do, run off?*

The house was quiet. There were two empty cups of cocoa on the table and glowing embers in the fireplace. Krys had left a blanket and a pillow on the couch.

Jeez, that fire must've been nice. I would've given anything to be here instead of there. How long was she gonna keep this shit up?

He sat down, kicked off his shoes, and turned over a piece of paper that was lying on the pillow. 'I love you Pops' was written in crayon. It was a good likeness of him. Krys was an angry green scribble in the background—*fucking Ceace—she sure got that right.*

GOOD MORNING

I was told to appreciate the simpler things, but Sarah is far from simple. I've never known someone so splintered and yet so whole.

Her left arm was bare, lying peacefully on the bed— A.C.A.B. The letters, tattooed in old English script— all cops are bastards.

I don't agree with that statement— what did Frankl say? good people placed in bad situations. I couldn't do it. I'd fucking kill somebody, but I appreciate the sentiment and where she comes from. She put herself through school— a single mother, a high school drop-out that'd sobered up and nailed a master's degree from a top-notch institution. She's as solid as they come—crazier than fuck, but the best lover I've ever had.

He purposely shut the closet door— the action louder than necessary. She didn't move.

They say you often become what you know— Sarah's a therapist, dealing with addicts and women at risk, and on the other side of the bed, I'm a shit-talking con man who pushes a God I don't believe in. Oh well, night and day.

He kicked one of her boots— it bounced rudely against the wall.

I've heard people thank the program for their lives and their jobs and their wives. But I was breathing before I got sober, I had a job of sorts, and I'd been married before. The program gave me none of those things, but what it did give me— after I woke up, was an ability to appreciate what I had— he pulled the curtain to the side and let the sunlight fall into her eyes— *and what I had lost.*

He sat beside her and ran his fingers down her arm— *come on baby, wake up.*

She opened one eye. "—You know, one of us likes to sleep."

He kissed her forehead. "Too much, you really should be up at this hour."

"Oh, did the little baby miss his mommy?"

"Come on sweetheart, you know that creeps me out."

She sat up and took the coffee cup from his hand. "What are you reading?"

"It's a Marcus Aurelius morning— I'm learning to detach."

"Fuck that—" She kicked the book from his hand. It sailed into the dresser— its pages crumpled and splayed.

"What the fuck! If you didn't have that coffee in your mitt I'd kick your fucking sleeping ass."

She laughed— her gold tooth flashing in the morning light. "—I wish you would, mommy needs a good ass-kicking."

"I'm not in that kind of mood."

She let the blanket slide down her body— naked, she teased him. "—and what kind of mood are you in, Daddy?"

He pulled the covers over her. She was consigned to his lack of interest. "—I met a new kid last night. He seemed all right."

"Treatment?"

"No. He walked in off the street. His wife dumped him at the meeting."

"His wife? How old is this *kid*?"

"I don't know, thirty-something. I gave him a ride home." He stroked her hair. "—I was thinking about me."

"When aren't you?"

"You know my Annie was a baby when I got clean. This kid's got a little girl…"

She set the coffee cup on the end table and slid closer to him— put her hand on his chest. "You can't save the world sweetheart."

"I didn't give a fuck about anybody. I put my daughter in danger. I fucked over my wife… "

"Okay—" She sat up straight, tied her hair in a knot upon her head. Her neck was normally a target for his lips but he was blinded by the past. "—is this what we're doing this morning, morbid self-reflection? It's a little too early for that crap."

"I gotta go see her today."

"Annie? I thought she was up north."

"No. My mother."

She got out of bed and pulled on a pair of skinny jeans. He didn't watch her dress. "I don't know why you just don't call. You're screwed up for days after going over there."

"I owe her. I can't repay what I put her through— I've told you that."

"I know baby, but for how long? There's got to be a limit."

"You know, one day I asked her how she dealt with me— the fights, the cops, our house getting vandalized, and she said that she laid in bed at night and prayed that I wouldn't die."

"I thought you didn't come from a religious family."

"I didn't"— he touched the crucifix hanging around his neck. "—I don't think she even believes in God."

"Well, at least you have that in common."

COURT CARD

He waited on the courthouse steps— a vicious Latin bird preening his feathers in the sun. He couldn't cross left to 8th, or right to Gold Street, but the courthouse was on neutral ground, so he had nothing to fear.

It's not like I give a fuck anyway— fucking Gold Street putos *are too busy cranking each other in the ass.*

He took a bite of his Icey.

If it wasn't for my brother, I wouldn't be here— fucking Grover. Two years gone, a victim of the tar. I don't fuck around with that shit. It's weak. The vatos *on the dope aren't good for much— and the go-fast, Ay Cabrón!. Lock up your fucking trash cans, the two-wheeled gangsters have arrived.*

Two street cops glanced his way and moved on.

Tina was my brother's ATM, hustling pussy to keep her and Grover well. She was living with him when he died— slumped in his chair, hands finally at peace in his lap. His last years were nothing but existence. A fucking waste, man. She cleaned up after that— stopped getting loaded, and after a year or so, it seemed right that she got with me. Eddie doesn't like it, neither does Blanca, but fuck her, man. She was out of line. It's none of her fucking business what Tina used to do.

He could hear her coming— the angry click-click-click of her come-fuck-me boots told the story.

"Fucking bitch. I'm lucky she didn't violate me."

"I told you, baby."

"Yeah, you're always telling me something, aren't you? Give me a lick of that ice cream." She put the tip in her mouth and closed her eyes. "Mmmm."

He jerked it away. "—What the fuck are you doing?"

She laughed as she wiped her lips with the back of her hand. "You gotta go with me."

"Where?"

"Fucking twelve-step, I gotta get this fucking card signed."

"Sign it yourself. Jesse never went one fucking time."

They walked down the steps and crossed against the light— heavy traffic strangled the downtown streets.

"I can't sign it, and neither can you. She told me exactly where to go. I think she's been there."

"Oh, a fucking alky P.O. huh?"

They stopped at a mini-mart— lottos, phone cards, and cold beer. Tina riffled through the candy as Albert pulled a 40 from the cooler.

"I think she might be, Beto. I thought I smelt booze on her breath."

"Nah, she probably just knows you." He opened the bottle and took a drink—*this is where it's at, man, fuck that other shit, those fucking guys doing dope— it's not necessary.*

The clerk jumped the counter with a small wooden bat. "—Hey, you guy— you pay for that."

Albert stared him down and tossed the twist cap over his shoulder; he took another pull. "Pay? Maybe— if I fucking feel like it."

"I call police now."

Albert smiled— a switchblade grin exposed his heart. "Call 'em— I'll burn this fucking rice paddy to the ground… with you in it."

The clerk had seen thugs like Albert before— if they didn't scatter when you barked, they surely bit. He stood his ground but didn't push the issue.

"Beto, what the fuck, man. You can't be drinking that."

"No, *you* can't." He took another heavy slug. "*I'm* not getting a fucking card signed." He winked at the clerk and pointed his finger against his temple and pulled the trigger. "—Five fucking dollars for this shit?" He let the bottle fall from his grasp. It shattered on the floor. "—It's all yours, *chinito*."

They left without paying.

MOMMY DEAREST

The air was stale and dog-breath heavy— the light diffused; the yellowed shades drawn. The house had neither been dusted nor vacuumed in years. She'd had a maid service— a Mother's Day gift, but she'd cut them loose. She said they were nosy and messing around in her cupboards. A toy poodle with mange and a pink jeweled collar growled from its perch on the dining room table. His mother was in her usual place— a recliner by the sliding glass door which was muddied by trails of sliding paw prints begging entrance to the home. On her left leg a calf-high stocking was slumped in disgust. Her right foot was bare and being used to rub the back of a Frankensteined mutt lying prostrate at her feet. He kissed her forehead. "Hey, Mom."

She replied without lifting her eyes. "Hi, Sweetheart."

"You got your program on?"

She attempted to turn the television down, but it got louder. "Yeah, it's uh... always... crap."

He used her remote to lower the volume.

She was wearing a flowered house coat— one he remembered from years past. It was thread worn and stained, but the red ribbon tied in her hair gave a nod to fashion— it accented the blotches on her skin. She was obese.

"I don't like that Johnny Ross." She looked James over. "—You're getting fat."

James laughed but years of emotional abuse wasn't easy to shake. "I can't stop eating."

"Well, you should. You're too good looking to be that big." There was a greasy bag of fast-food on the table and a sixty-ounce-soda sweating on the bar. "—Doesn't Sandy take care of you?"

"It's Sarah and yes, she's great to me."

"I thought you were married to Sandy. Where is she?"

His wedding picture was on a shelf by the television— his first wife.

"I haven't seen her in years, mom."

"You divorced her? Your father and I were together for thirty-seven years. We never had a day of trouble."

"She died, mom— you remember."

She closed her eyes and rubbed the dog with her foot. "—I guess I do— not pretty, was it? Maybe you can use her as an example in one of your talks. You still go to those classes don't you?"

"Yeah."

"I would've thought that you'd be better by now— you know your father was stronger than that. He could take or leave his liquor. Could you get me a water?"

James walked into the kitchen. Dirty dishes were piled on the counter. He watched a line of ants descend to the floor— his gaze traveling across gravy stains and claw marks before landing on a soiled circular rug protecting cheap vinyl tiles. The carpet stunk.

What the fuck was that toy? God-damn-it, it was my favorite... a Roll Boy Racer, that's what it was. I used to run it right here— up and down the kitchen. I remember my father tripping over it— breaking one of the wheels. He was plastered— pounding the Cutty Sark and arguing with my mother. I got kicked in the stomach for his blind drunkenness. My mom did nothing to stop him— better me than her I guess. Shit, when he kicked me I threw up on his leg. I got beat double for that mess.

He grabbed a dish cloth and turned the water on— it was as hot as he could stand. It burned his hands if he didn't move fast.

Sometimes it feels good to hurt— sharp physical pain to deaden emotional trauma— a sprinkling of hot bacon grease, a razor blade, a piece of broken glass. I don't cut myself bad enough to scar anymore, but I do enjoy the occasional escape from the moment.

"Leave 'em!" She yelled from the living room. "I'll do 'em when I get up."

He ignored her. It was at least a week's worth. When he finished he filled a glass with water and delivered her drink.

"I guess you got to know your limitations, don't you sweetheart."

"Yeah, I guess I do." He gave his mother another kiss. "I gotta go mom— just wanted to stop by and tell you I love you."

She held on to his arm, her fingers bent imitations of his own with chipped red polish.

"I love you too sweetheart. You were always my favorite— never gave me a moment of trouble—" She picked up the remote; the volume rose. "—tell Sandy I love her."

As he walked to his car, he wondered if the last day that he walked from this house would ever come. He stepped over his name, carved years ago into the wet sidewalk cement. He sat in his car and lit a half-burnt cigar.

Sandy and I were married when I was twenty-four. She was eighteen— more girl than woman. We'd met at a house party a few years before. I was obsessed with her. If I close my eyes, I can still trace the pattern of the freckles on her cheeks— the big dipper exploding into the sea green galaxy of her eyes. As most good things were, it seemed perfect at the time, and then the time changed and the drugs and the alcohol climbed into our bed and it got ugly and deceitful and violent and I never wondered how I could be so obsessed with someone, and yet so willing to risk her devotion by sleeping with women that would never be her equal. How many of her lovers did I assault? My payback for cheating on her. There were the two in the bar that night, the cop on the beach, the old pervert at the gas station— a string of victims, random men used like tools to hurt me. And then, the restraining orders, the suicide attempts, the unanswered prayers of intercession came to play. There was rarely a day without drama. I remember the blisters breaking out on my hands— yellow stress-filled pockets of pus collecting on my fingers. The doctors told me that something needed to change, but I refused to let go— I couldn't. In the end, something broke, and I didn't give a fuck who she slept with. I got clean, and it was as if she died, and then she did. I remember the phone call from her mother— her voice trembling through loss; Sandy had overdosed in a motel room. I was devastated, but that night I slept well. I finally knew where she was.

NOT THAT EASY

The family was at the dinner table— chicken strips, mac n cheese, and a Jello salad. They were C.C.'s favorites. The meal was civil, the f-word count at a minimum, but tension crept around the corners of the room like soft thunder on the horizon.

"Chet in sales says it's gonna be cool. Mr. Grant was pissed, but he likes me, says we all fuck up— sorry Ceace, screw up sometimes."

C.C. laughed— *she was resilient, untouched.*

"Jacob, *you* know it's not cool right?"

"Yeah, of course. I meant at work." He winked at his little girl. "I got a sponsor last night. We're working steps and stuff. He said I got a good attitude. Meeting makers make it."

"Are you going to a meeting tonight?"

"I was thinking I'd hang back with you guys— do like a movie thing or something. Would you like that, Ceace?"

"Can we—"

"She wants you to go to a meeting. We'll drop you off after dinner."

C.C. scrunched up her nose and bit the tail off a dinosaur chicken strip. She walked the amputee reptile through a white tarpit of cool ranch dressing.

Jacob stood in the bathroom with the door open. He would've gone outside to call but every time he walked away, Krys followed him. She didn't trust him.

It's not like I was cheating. I got drunk— I wasn't swimming under some girl's skirt.

The large 12 on the business card was easy to read, but the phone number, not so much: 714-794-5625.

What the hell was that bottom line? 'Making Your Business My Business.' I sure hope not.

He hit the speaker button and set the phone down as he checked his look in the mirror.

"Speak to me."

"James? It's Jacob."

"What's up, my man? Still hanging?"

"Yeah, it's going good. I didn't lose my job."

"Yet…"

"What do you mean, yet? Come on dude, don't be a dick."

"I'm just fucking with you. I'm glad. You got a chance to straighten things up— show 'em who you really are."

Krystal stood in the bedroom listening to the call. She didn't want to, but she felt better when she did.

"Are you gonna be at that meeting tonight?"

"Yeah, I'm the coffee guy— no coffee, no serenity. If the coffee makers went on strike the fucking meetings would crumble."

"So, that's a yes?"

"A big yes. Were you thinking of going? It's participation tonight."

"What does that mean?" *Fuck, is that a grey hair?* He plucked it out.

"It means we all get a shot to share— if you want to."

"What if I don't want to?" Jacob held the offending strand up to the light. "Can't I just listen?"

"I'd prefer it if you did— you ever see *Gilligan's Island?*"

"Yeah."

"And you know what a newcomer is, right?"

"I'm a newcomer."

"Exactly. *Gilligan's Island*: seven newcomers that couldn't get off a fucking island. A bunch of crazy schemes— coconut rocket launchers, and all sorts of whacky shit, but they couldn't fix a fucking boat. They should've flown in somebody with time to tell 'em how to get home."

Jacob laughed. "—I'll keep my mouth shut."

"Not with me, you won't. It's my job to listen to you and offer suggestions based on my experience— if I don't have experience, maybe I can hook you up with someone that does. But in the rooms it's different. We know how to wreck cars, fuck up marriages, and go to jail. We know how to drink and get high— you can't tell us nothing about that. We've done that life."

"Yeah, I get it man. Good talk, dude. I save the drama for you— how bout you just sign my card and I'll kick it with the fam?"

"Look, smartass. You get down there and I'll give you a ride home. Meet me at 6:30. You can help out— be my coffee apprentice."

"It's almost 6:00 now—" Krystal grabbed her sweater and told C.C. to get in the car. "—I still gotta take a shower and stuff."

"Come dirty. I'll see you there— *ciao*."

Krystal had her purse on her shoulder and her car keys in her hand.

"—Let's go. Ceace and I will drop you off."

Jacob hesitated.

"We're in the car." She walked out leaving the front door open. He followed.

Krystal watched as Jacob kissed C.C. goodbye— *he thinks I'm the problem.* She followed him with her eyes— counting each breath, as he walked into the hall. He had a stagger in his step. It wasn't from the accident. The cut on his lip hadn't hindered his mouth. His leg was fine.

I used to wait on the front steps for my father. Some days he was almost nice to me. He'd put his hand on my head— never a kiss or a squeeze or a hug, but sometimes a touch. Most days he would just pass by without acknowledgement— and always a stagger to his step, a list to one side like a great alcoholic ship taking in water as it fought its way to shore. I was terrified and needy— craving his attention and dreading the thought of his touch. I remember the broken glass, my mother's screams, and the muffled pillow-talk of her beatings. I wanted to save her from his rage, but I couldn't. I was no one.

"Mom?" C.C. put her hand on Krystal's shoulder. "He's in."

"I know, Ceace. I saw him."

NEW LODGINGS IN HELL

The homework was done. The dinner dishes washed and put away, the beds made, the dogs fed. Britney was quietly reading in her room. Bridget was cuddled next to her father. A once unknown feeling of peace pervaded the house. The evening was just fine without her.

*****

Bayside was a rehab on the outskirts of town. It sat on a cliff overlooking the harbor. The clients— that's what they liked to be called, were from a stratum of society that most people never knew. These were the privileged ones. The ones that dabbled in cocaine and drank natural wines— unlike MD 20/20 or the noxious Night Train, their beverages had actually seen a grape at one time. If Connie was an alcoholic of a lesser variety, she might've been housed in a county facility— a woman's institution that looked down on "crazy bitches that spoke with their fists." To Bayside's credit, it offered the occasional scholarship opportunity to those that could never afford admittance.

There was a circle of chairs arranged in a group room— thirteen clients and a rehab facilitator gathered for a meeting. The facilitator's name was Regina. She was a recovered alcoholic who was short on patience. She'd had enough of entitled adult children demanding preferential treatment when, in her opinion, what they really needed was a thorough ass-whipping.

"Settle up now— let's start with the serenity prayer. God..."

The group joined in unison— as close as one might expect.

"Okay, let's go around the room and identify ourselves— starting on my left."

"I'm Hector, and I'm an alcoholic."

"Brandon, alcoholic."

"Lyndsey, addict."

"I'm Franklin, and I'm a garbage pail." The twenty-something white boy was wearing a Fila track suit and had his hair in corn-row braids. The group laughed but Regina threw heavy shade in his direction. She wasn't in the mood to play.

"Franklin, addict, alcoholic."

"I'm Mathias Buxton Brown— alcoholic."

"Connie, visitor."

"I'm Tony, I'm—"

"Hold up, Tony." Regina swept back to Connie. "—A visitor? Who exactly are you visiting, Connie?"

"Well, technically I'm not visiting anyone. I'm a guest of the facility."

"A guest?"

"Did I stutter?" Connie rolled her eyes. "I'm a guest. Non-alcoholic, and I'm surely not a fucking garbage pail—" She leaned forward in her chair and turned toward Franklin. "—you *are* aware that you're white aren't you?"

"Connie."

She turned back to Regina.

"You're the one he's making fun of, not me," She pursed her lips and with her left pinky finger touched the crease of her mouth. "—you know my situation. I'm forced to be here. Why don't you stop being a bitch and help somebody? That's what you're here for, right?"

"Yes Connie, that's right. I'm here to help somebody. Tony, would you like to continue?"

CAN I GET A SIDE OF FRIES WITH THAT?

The alcoholics swarmed the diner. The booths jammed with those in recovery. They were loud— joyful, laughing and cursing; mixing it up like children at play— come to me as a child, the Master had said, and they did.

"You'd think they'd find us a bother, but most of us tip heavy— survivors of shipwrecks usually do. We walk on the sunny side of the street and our gratitude shows. The diner likes our business and we treat them with respect."

James had a line for everything. A fucking zebra could run through the room and he'd put meaning behind it.

On the way in, they stopped to pay their respects to Alan and his crew— the Wizards, that's what James called them; six or seven older men and women, out past their bedtime, holding court at table eight.

Jacob and James sat at a table in the center of the room.

"That's about three hundred years of recovery sitting over there— could you imagine?"

"No offense, dude, but I'm not as thrilled with it as you are— if I'm still sitting here when I'm that old, shoot me. How often do you do this shit?"

"I don't think Cindy would like you calling her Pancake Palace 'shit.'"

"I meant the meetings."

A woman kissed James on the cheek. She was another one of those not-like-a-drunk drunks— business attire, beautiful, long braided hair.

"Thanks for doing that for me, baby."

"No problem, Tish. Hey, Sarah wants you to call— something about the uh—"

"Who's this?" She turned her attention to Jacob.

"That's Jacob. He was just telling me how much he can't stand us."

"I was not."

She laughed. "Don't listen to a fucking thing he says, Jacob... this man is out of his mind." She kissed James again, gave him a big squeeze. "—he's certifiable."

She walked away.

"That's what we call negative love— now why you hating on the diner?"

"I love the diner— and you're an asshole for throwing me under the bus— what the fuck, man? I like you guys. I just don't like the meetings." Jacob reached for a menu. "—You go every day? Twenty something years and you still gotta go?"

"It's thirty, and I don't *have* to go. I *want* to." James pushed back his hair. "—I enjoy these people. I care about their lives. And, at the risk of being crass, I benefit from this shit. Do you know how much money my newfound ability to keep my mouth shut has made me?"

"Hold up, did you just say *you* keep your mouth shut?"

"Let's just say I'm not telling my boss to fuck off these days. Let me ask you something. How much did your last debauch cost you? Your truck's fucked up— you got a lawyer, right? What are you looking at, a few thousand dollars to get straightened out?"

"Yeah, about that, maybe a little more."

"Okay, so your decisions are costing you. My decisions enrich me. You're beating around like I'm a slave to this shit. I'm not. When I was drinking, I went nowhere. I was chained to my illness— incapable of stepping up. I'm not the slave at this table. I'm not the one who's getting dropped off at the meeting by his mommy."

"And you go every day?"

"Oh, you little fucker. All right. Let me tell you something, let's talk about motivation. You don't wanna go to these meetings, do you?"

"No."

"But you're willing to do it now because the heat's on, right?"

"What do you mean?"

"I'm guessing your wife's had enough— you sleeping in the same bed?"

"Couch."

"Right, so here's how this works." James stood up and pushed his chair to the side. "You go out, and you fuck up— in your case, plowing head-first into the shit— or a parked car if you will, and now your wife's furious— this is the heat we're talking about. You get a drunk driving or whatever and your job is on the line... more heat."

As he was speaking, James backed away— a step at a time, slow, deliberate moves.

"You might be on a court-card, or have to drug test—" he took another step in retreat. "—you're not drug testing are you?"

"No."

"Okay, so the heat's on... and you don't wanna get burned, so you'll do anything you can to move away from that flame, to get them to shut the fuck up and leave you alone. You back away— like going to those fucking meetings, and getting your card signed, and staying sober— being a good boy, and after a while, when you've been playing it straight, things cool down. The heat disappears."

James was a good six feet from the table. "And now, your motivation to stay sober is gone. They're no longer mad at work—" He took a step towards Jacob. "—your court-card is filled—" Another step. "—your wife pulls back the covers and lets that little white ass of yours slide back up into the big bed." Two more steps.

James moved toward the table until he was standing breath-close to Jacob. "—And now, your motivation to stay sober— to not get burned, is gone... and you slowly drift back toward that incendiary moment. And then one day— lacking the motivation to stay clean—" James lifted a glass of water off the table. "—you pick up a drink, and you get burned all over again."

There was a burst of applause from the room. James bowed and returned to his chair. He lowered the volume.

"Sadly, Jacob, this cycle will repeat over, and over, and over, until you've lost your job, and your wife, and basically everything you love, and then one day you'll do it again and you'll die."

He took a sip of water.

"Look kid, you told me that you were sober before, and I bet you only did enough to not get burned. Am I right?"

"Yeah, putting it that way, I guess I did."

The waitress took their order— two coffees and a tapioca pudding for James.

"So, if I wanted to stay sober, what should I do?"

"You turn your back on the heat and you walk away. You head toward an ideal. You'll never reach perfection— none of us can. The only thing we do perfectly is not drink one day at a time, but we strive to be better across the board— better employees, friends, fathers, and husbands— servants to those we love. We don't back away from the heat; we turn, and walk toward the light."

"And how do I do that?"

"Well, the first step is believing that you're gonna get burned again— conceding to your innermost self that you're fucked, that no matter what you do to get better, you're going again, and you don't have the power to stop it. You gotta come from a place of desperation."

"But what if I do what you say?"

"Lots of guys follow orders, Jacob. It's called compliance. But compliance doesn't mean recovered. You need a shift in thinking or consciousness."

"And you can give me that?"

"Jacob, if I could do that, my father would still be alive, as would my nephew, and my first wife. They all three came here on court cards— backing away from the heat, and they all died."

"So why should I do this shit— sitting here with you, going to these meetings? If it doesn't work, why bother?"

James stared into a spoonful of whip-cream topping. He was trying to capture the essence of the moment that changed him— "Because just maybe, if you walk this path, you'll wake up. You'll see the truth— you'll hit bottom. And I'm not talking about circumstance— the shit-show that you've created of your life. I'm talking about a condition of heart— a moment when you break and your self-sufficiency fails. A moment where you reach out to something beyond your realm of existence, and then you and I will never have to have this conversation again."

The waitress set a piece of lemon pie at Jacob's place. "It's from table eight— the old guy in the bright pink coveralls."

DOUBLE-SCRUB

Go ahead, call it a trashy romance novel— and you'd be right, but if you had to do sixty days in this Bayside castle of forced god integration you'd be sitting right beside me, hiding in these pages, and trying not to remember that you still had fifty-three days to go before you escaped the evil clutches of Mistress Regina. I'm on a twin bed for Christ's sake— twenty thread count sheets, and my fucking kids aren't answering the phone. This, sugar, is what's known as hell.

Connie turned the page— Dwaine had taken Sasha by force; he'd ravaged her in an upstairs room in the castle.

Ravaged, that's a word I haven't heard in a while. It isn't in Robert's vocabulary. The last time we had sex was in May, or maybe March— I caught him jerking off in the garage.

Regina walked into the room without a courtesy knock. "What's happening, princess?"

"I'm not answering to that."

She ran her hand across the opposite bed. "—Still empty, huh?"

Connie ignored her. Maybe she'd go away.

"I heard you were complaining about breakfast again— not to your liking?"

She opened a cupboard and found what she was looking for—

contraband. She unfolded a plastic grocery bag.

"What do you think you're doing? That's my stuff."

Regina swept the contents of the cupboard into the bag. "I'm taking it. It doesn't belong here. Where do you think you are?"

Connie got to her feet. "—I'm in hell. You can't take my make-up. That's expensive— more than you make in a month."

The room was tight. Regina had a few pounds on her.

This bitch looks like she can handle herself— probably try to pull some of that poor-side-of-town-bullshit on me. Black and proud and can't wait until she can put an incapacitated little white girl in her place. I should slap her Jheri-curled attitude back to Hayward or wherever the hell she came from.

"We're going to an outside meeting tonight."

"Then give me my fucking make-up."

"You can go as is, or you can stay here."

"Fine. I'll stay here—" Connie flopped down on the bed.

"Good choice, Princess. I think Richard is going to double-scrub the kitchens and the toilets. I'm sure he can use your help."

"Fuck you. I'm not doing that."

Regina calmly sat on the unoccupied bed. She smiled at Connie. "Princess."

"Stop fucking calling me that."

"You're court ordered to be here. What was that, your third assault charge? Your Daddy paid—"

"He's my husband, and I paid for this with my own money."

"And what job was that— they pay you to go to spas and get your lips done? Your *Daddy* spent a lot of money to keep you out of jail."

"What do you think *this* is? You're a fucking guard, Regina. How about I get you fired? You can't come in here and call me names."

"Princess, I don't think you have any idea of what I can do. Bayside has an excellent relationship with the courts. You can continue acting like the world is here to serve you, and I can call your case manager, and tell her that you're unwilling to do as asked. You will be out of here, and in jail, before you can say, 'I don't eat gluten.' Now, you can go to the meeting, or you can scrub toilets, it's your call."

A voice called from outside. "—Regina?"

"Yeah, in here, Bill."

A tall orderly wearing Bayside greys entered the room. He placed a grocery bag of clothes on the unoccupied bed. A large, masculine-looking woman with facial tattoos and a glass eye stood behind him. She looked like she'd done hard time.

"Princess, this is Emily— one of our scholarship clients. She'll be rooming with you. Do us a favor and help her get acclimated."

MEETING TIME

She was wearing a tight black dress— sleeveless, the tattoos on her arms breathing under the low-watt light. Albert walked into the bathroom with a beer in his hand. He kissed her neck. "Where you going, *Pollita*?"

"We're going to that meeting."

"Not me."

"You said you'd go."

He held up his 40. "Can I bring this?"

She looked him over, her eyes smokey brown under thick lashes and drawn on brows. Her lips, black lined, deep red. "You don't give a fuck about me, Beto. I don't know why you keep me here."

"Don't give me that bullshit." His brother's name was tattooed on her neck. He traced it with his finger and then wrapped his hand in her hair, pulled her head back, exposing her throat. "—Fuck me and I'll go."

"You're so full of shit— like a fucking little boy. Stay home then." She adjusted her bra. "—I'm going. I'm sure if you're not with me, I can find somebody to keep me company."

He tagged her with a hard right slap to her face. She dropped to her knees— a puppet hanging unconscious off the end of his arm— his hand wrapped in her hair. He let her drop. "I fucking told you I'd go."

They walked through the back door into the kitchen— Jacob leading the way as if he were walking into a bar, Krystal drifting warily concerned behind him. There were two large pots of coffee on the counter. They'd been ready to go an hour before the meeting. James believed that a hot coffee and a kind word should wait for anyone who chose to attend— especially the new ones.

"Hey, James, what's happening? This is Krystal."

I wish I could say that this was a first— a newcomer bringing his wife to the meeting, or a wife bringing her husband, or a mother, father, or children, but I've seen this a thousand times. These visitors are the ones who pay for the alcoholic's seat in these rooms —'an illness of this sort… involves those about us in a way that no other human sickness can.'

James smiled as he shook her hand. "You're still hanging with this guy? It must be date night."

"Come on, dude. Don't be a jerk." Krystal laughed at Jacob's discomfort. "I wanted her to see what I'm doing." He picked a towel off the floor and hung it on a rack.

"Oh, really?" James removed the destined-for-the trash rag and tossed it. "—and what *are* you doing?"

Jacob put his hand on Krystal's shoulder. "—I told you he could be like this."

She subtly shook him off and moved toward James. "—I guess I'm not the only one who wonders what you're up to."

"All right kids… " James laughed. "Easy does it and all that crap. We're just having fun. Krystal, you've got a good man there, and it's a pleasure to meet you."

"You too, James, and now I have a face to put with the name."

Sarah walked into the kitchen, gorgeous in a dark grey pantsuit and black leather boots.

"Well, look who it is," James kissed her on the cheek. "You're gonna have to be on Jacob's team."

Sarah smiled as she shook Jacob's hand. "I sure hope you're getting him straightened out."

"I'm trying, but it ain't easy. How do you deal with him?"

Sarah laughed and gave James a kiss. "You just have to love him more than you want to beat his ass." She winked at Krystal. "I gotta go, sweetheart. Love you."

He followed her with his eyes. He never tired of watching her move.

"Hello?" Jacob tapped James's shoulder. "Are you with us?"

"Leave it, Jacob. I remember when you used to look at me like that."

"I still do, come on, Krys."

James turned to Krystal— "in his defense she is intoxicating…. are you one of us— can I call you, Krys?"

"Yeah, sure. That's what Jacob calls me. I'm not one of you guys, but my father was an alcoholic."

"Mine too. You gotta love those Jack Daniel's moments, eh?"

"My dad was a vodka man. He said they couldn't smell it on him."

"Ah, a true aficionado of deceit. Is he still around?"

"No."

"I'm sorry to hear that." He pulled back a touch, noticing the flash of hurt in Krystal's eyes. "—Well, you're gonna love my Sarah.

"She's speaking?"

"Yes, Jacob, and in honor of, I'm giving you the night off." James put his hand on his protégé's shoulder. "Why don't you guys go get a couple of seats? This place is gonna fill up."

Tina and Albert parked on the street and walked up the path. The slap had been forgotten, if not forgiven, being as it was a common and accepted occurrence. He put his hand around her waist. She tightened, but didn't pull away.

"You know most men wouldn't go with you—" He stepped onto the grass and pulled her along. He pushed her back against a tree and put his hand on the inside of her thigh. "—open it."

She spread her legs for him as his hand traveled further.

"Beto we got to go—"

"I'm doing an hour for you; you got a minute for me."

Two nondescript white vans pulled into the lot. The headlights slicing across the trees as they parked. The doors slid back and a clean-faced Connie stepped out followed by Emily and her fellows.

"This place is a shit-hole." Connie felt exposed without her make-up. The young girl next to her reached into her pocket and pulled out a tube of lip-gloss— she liberally applied the product.

"Where did you get that?" She ignored Connie. "I don't think you're supposed to have that. Regina was pretty clear on the rules."

The girl's friend took a hit off a vape and blew a large cloud at Connie— the bitch of Bayside, they called her. "Dry up, grannie."

"Look, you little slut—"

The two girls walked toward the meeting, leaving an agitated Connie in their wake.

She knocked on the driver's side of the van— the window was open, Bill, the orderly was playing a game on his phone. "—That brown-haired girl has make-up."

He stared blindly, and silently, in Connie's direction as the electric window rose.

A full house— about two hundred recovering alcoholics filled the club. Krystal and Jacob found seats on the aisle.

"He's fun."

"What do you mean?"

"By the way you talked about the diner I thought this was gonna be a bunch of old men in trench coats. His wife's beautiful."

"Look at that guy, he looks like a fucking skeleton."

"Jacob!" She laughed besides his rudeness.

"He does— James said he got sober when he was twenty. What's that, like, a hundred years?"

Albert and Tina found seats in the back.

"Weren't you supposed to drop your card off?

"I didn't see a sign."

"Well, you better get it counted."

An elderly grey-haired woman sitting in the row behind them leaned forward— "Were you speaking of a court card?"

Tina stayed silent. Albert turned around. "Yeah, you take them?"

"Do you see the woman near the front door— sitting at the table? If you take it to her after the meeting she'll sign you up."

"How much is it?"

"It's free, sweetheart. Are you new?"

"Do I look new?"

"No, not you, dear."

The room settled. The group said their prayer and then, after a short reading, a few of those in attendance stepped to the lectern, and read sections from a dark blue book. A robust applause welcomed Sarah. She took her place on the podium.

"Hi. I'm Sarah and I'm an alcoholic—"

"Hi, Sarah!"

"—and if the coffee is bad. I know who to blame."

She took a sip of water and launched in. "My father was an alcoholic. I went to my first family support meeting when I was ten years old. How do you explain to a little girl why her daddy chose alcohol over her?"

Krystal squeezed Jacob's arm.

"I was in and out of jail starting at thirteen. I never had a boyfriend my age. I met my husband during a drug deal. He was brilliant, tall, good-looking, and we got married while he was in prison. We had three children, and our neighbors were terrified of us. Every so often, one of us would get sent to twelve-step, and the other would follow."

Albert was listening— she was pretty, and he wondered what kind of drugs they were selling. Tina played with her phone.

"I thought you were lames. I would sit in the back row, arms crossed, listening to your bullshit, knowing that it didn't work. You guys couldn't save my dad. He died drunk."

She took another sip.

"But there's a funny thing that happens around here— my sponsor, Winnie, often refers to it. It's when a new person comes to these rooms— walled up, obstinate as one can be, like I was, and then they hear a word, or a slight innocuous little phrase, and it slips past those walls and it touches their heart.

"There was a man in a meeting that I used to attend. He never made a lick of sense, but then one day he said that we all have a little golden person inside, and I heard him."

Albert leaned forward— *a memory of himself as a young boy, a bluebird drawn on a page, a grandmother smiling down upon him, a sense of pride in accomplishment—* he was her golden boy.

The thought sickened him. He looked away from Sarah, and grabbed Tina's phone. He scrolled through her photos seeking comfort, but there was none to be found. The boy had been displaced— a cruel, evil man in his stead, a beast that his grandmother would detest. And always, a bottle in his hand and the pale dull glow of inebriation seeping from him. He was nothing like that boy. He was unrecognizable.

Sarah put her hands on the podium, holding herself in place.

"I was a little girl who just wanted her daddy to love her, and when alcohol took him away, I took my anger out on the world. And it's a strange thing, that even though I hated his drinking more than anything I ever hated in my life, I too became entangled with the love of that poison, and the effect it gave me."

When she finished speaking, Albert and Tina took the card to get signed. The meeting wasn't yet over— there were announcements being read, but he'd had enough.

Fuck them, if they want more than that. Tina was here for the talking bit— the bullshit. I know how this crap works— fucking carny tricks. The things they say upset anyone. It's made like that.

The clients from Bayside had also made their way toward the door. It'd been one of the longest hours in Connie's life.

I should have scrubbed toilets— an alkie in an off-the-rack pantsuit crying about her daddy. Jail has got to be better than this. That place Martha Stewart was in looked pretty nice— badminton and beef Bordeaux.

Krystal met Sarah in the reception line. "I really enjoyed your speech."

"You're welcome. It's Krystal, right? I'm sorry I didn't get the formal introduction earlier. How are you?"

"Pissed off."

"At least you recognize it."

"It's kind of hard not to when your husband's such an asshole."

Sarah glanced unconsciously at the long line.

"Oh, I'm sorry. I just wanted to say, thank you."

"No, don't be sorry. Do you have a phone?"

Krystal pulled a bedazzled phone from her bag— jewels flashing under fluorescent light.

"Call me—" Sarah gave her the number. "—are you up late?"

"Lately, yeah."

"I'll be home in an hour. If I don't answer, leave a message. I'll hit you back."

GOD CALLING

Albert barely missed a passing car as they pulled onto the parkway. "Beto! What the fuck, man?"

"I didn't see 'em." He straightened his line. "*Ay Cabrón.*"

"You okay?"

"When I was a *niño*, I didn't like getting sick. If I felt like something was gonna come up I'd swallow it."

"Are you sick??"

"No, it was that fucking woman, talking all that shit— those stories. I'm not sick, but it feels like I'm choking something down, yeah— too much thinking."

"Do you want me to drive?"

"No, but… do you think I'm a good boy?"

"Dude, you're freaking me out, man. What the fuck are you saying?"

"My *tita* used to call me her good boy."

"You're fucking tripping, babe" She spotted a liquor store on the corner, the word 'sale' flying in big red print. "—pull up, ey. I'll get us something."

Albert sat in the car as Tina went inside. He looked at his hands— fresh cuts across his knuckles, old teeth scars like wedding bands beneath the ink.

I was raised by my grandparents— a drunk and a saint. My tita was nothing but kind. She would hold me close to her heart, her strong arms around me, the scent of cinnamon in her hair. I remember the kitchen on 9th street, the afternoon conchas *cooling on the shelf. She used to buy my drawings— twenty-five cents for the small ones and a dollar for large. Her favorite was a bluebird that she taped to the wall above her bed. They buried her with that bird. The drawing was lying upon her chest. Her rosary was lying upon the bird. I put him on my neck. He's here to remind me."*

He reached up and stroked the tail.

She wouldn't have liked it placed that way on my body. I would have got a whipping for it.

There were boys in my neighborhood that would tease me for my clothes— hand stitched, that she had made. They jumped me one day. I remember their fists pummeling me as I tried to escape— crying, begging. I ran to my grandmother. She held me close and I felt safe there, but then... she pushed me away and said that I'd forgotten something when I ran. She said that even though I'd escaped, I'd left my pride and my manhood cowering in the schoolyard. I understood what she was saying, but at the time I was afraid to retrieve them.

My grandfather liked the bottle. He was a very mean man. When he died, I was surprised to see my grandmother weep. He was a coward who took his strength from the booze. He said it removed fear and revealed God. I thought the drink might help me. It did. One, two, three drinks, often more, and I grew. I never ran again. I taught those boys, catching them one at a time and showing them who I was. For every blow they had thrown, I threw four or five in return. When I got older, the violence served me and then school and honest work and honor slipped away. But my grandmother never stopped loving me, even when I knew I didn't deserve it.

I remembered the last day I looked in a mirror— that may sound strange to you now, but you didn't see my reflection. My face was hard, cold, unforgiving and the ink beneath my eye telegraphed intent. I was ashamed. The booze had tricked me. I wasn't brave. I was afraid. I knew what my grandmother would say— "What have you left behind, Albert? Where is my good boy?"

He didn't hear Tina return. She appeared in the car. "Motherfucker needs a beat down." She handed him a 40. He held it for a moment— weighed its worth, and then he laid it on the seat beside him.

"Fucking *chinito*, eye-fucking my titties." She smoothed her dress. Her breasts barely contained, her nipples like daggers set. She opened her beer and put her lips around the mouth of the bottle— a lover entreating the booze to cum.

He pulled back onto the road without taking a drink. As he drove, his right hand, like the hand of a clock, touched the 40 at his side, and the bluebird on his neck.

Their apartment was near the train station. They parked in the alley behind. Tina was a few feet from the car before she realized he wasn't following her. She went back for him. He rolled the window down.

"You okay, Beto?"

"I'm just sitting here. My stomach hurts."

"Don't shit yourself in the car." She laughed and walked up the stairs.

The 40 on the seat was no longer sweating. He had never let one sit so long. He slid his hand across the bottle, stared at the label —the words blurred, the paper pulling away from the glass. There was a crucifix hanging from his rearview mirror and a glow-in-the-dark Jesus— arms wide, fastened to his dashboard. He spoke to the figure.

"You been watching me, Man?" His hand played across the bottle. "—been watching this whole time?"

A light flickered from above. Tina was inside.

"I'm a fucking piece of work, huh?" There were tears crowding to the forefront of his eyes. "*Your* work. I bet you feel pretty good about that— making shit like me."

He opened the bottle, but didn't drink.

He thought of his grandfather, passed out on the floor in his dirty underpants, his grandmother covering him with a hand-sewn shawl.

"I can do whatever I want. You could've stopped me, but you didn't."

He held the bottle to his lips and laughed. "—I guess you didn't care for me, or them, did you? What's the count, huh? Did you get it all written down in your fucking ledger— let me see, Albert, a fucking chicken clucking down booze and strutting on the boulevard like he's a big man— there you go."

He flipped the open bottle into the air. The lukewarm beer splashed over the seats and carpet, bouncing to the floor.

"You fucking sat there, Man. Why didn't you stop me? Why didn't you make me be good?"

The tears fell. He hadn't the strength to retract them. He reached for the bottle on the floor, the contents now depleted. It was no use. The curtain was torn back. The lie exposed. He pulled the pistol from the glove box.

He was afraid.

"Just once, Jesus, for my grandmother's sake, show me who you are…" He put the barrel of the gun against his heart, his finger on the trigger. "I'm tired of being me."

*****

Emily was sitting on her bed in a pair of ill-fitting pajama bottoms and a loose silk blouse when Connie came back from snack. *Bayside's idea of a crème brulee was a caramel pudding and dairy free topping— at least the berries were fresh.* Connie had washed her face and settled her evening affairs. There had been no calls.

Emily waited until Connie laid down on her bed. "Do you want to pray with me?"

"Why?"

"To thank God for another day."

"Ha! No thanks." Connie rolled on to her side and faced the wall.

Emily got to her knees. "God, thank you for your blessings. Thank you for my life, for my daughter, and for my chance to start new. Thank you for Regina, and Dr. Plummer. Thank you for the path you've shown me—"

"Are you fucking kidding me?" Connie rolled over. "You can't take that outside? How many fucking 'thank yous' are on that list?"

Emily ignored her. "—thank you for the hardships in my life, thank you for my roommate Connie, bless her and her—"

"Look babe, I don't mind you praying. If I was you, I'd probably be talking to God too, but keep me out of it— and work on being aware that you're not the only one in here, okay?"

Emily stood and walked to the door. "Open or closed?"

"Do you snore?"

Emily laughed. "I don't know. I never slept with me."

"Close it— we wouldn't want anyone trying to get in here and take your virginity."

She closed the door and turned off the light. "I'm not a virgin. I have a daughter."

"Yeah, me too— two of them."

*****

He loved their stove—a slate blue Viking Pro. His mother had a 1970s Amana piece of shit, but when it came right down to it, a grilled cheese on raisin tastes just as good on a stove with only one working burner as it does on this monstrosity—*maybe it's the pan?*

Sarah walked in and kissed his forehead. "You getting that stove straightened out?"

"I wish everything I loved was this well behaved."

She took a seat at the counter. "—what do you think about that kid?"

"Who— Jacob?"

"I just got off the phone with Krystal. Do you think he's full of shit?"

He took a bite of the sandwich— the warm cheese stretching four or five inches before it broke and fell on his chin. He put the errant string in his mouth. "Sweetheart, can you get me that real large copper pan in the hallway?"

"Why?"

"I'm gonna fix you up a plate of mind your own fucking business."

"Come on, I'm serious— you got cheese on your pajamas."

She picked it off with her teeth— Gruyere with cotton fuzz.

"I don't know. Were you and I full of shit? Nobody would have put a fucking dime on either of us." He gave her a bite. "—Great talk by the way. I'm standing in the kitchen, listening to you, and realizing how lucky I am. Not only do I admire this woman, but I'm thrilled with her heart, and I'm fascinated with her intellect, and when I tire of those things, I get to take her into the bedroom, and fuck her brains out."

"Well, there goes the intellect— anyway, I was talking to Krystal."

"You're a broken record, baby."

"I know, it's just that we talked about this before, when the husband is checking in with you, and the wife's checking in with me."

"We stay out of other people's business."

"Yeah, I know. But you've been doing this longer than I have. You're better at this than I am."

He put the plate in the sink— sprayed it down. He was fanatical when it came to a clean kitchen.

"Sarah, you know that's not true. I've just had more practice. Look, Jacob could be full of shit— he probably is and doesn't even know it, but Krystal could be full of shit too. We're not therapists— well, you are, but I'm not. We stick to our experience. We let the two of them figure it out. You can suggest outside help, and you can be kind, but that's it. We don't play God. Now, why don't you get your ass in that bedroom and give me a naughty spanking for being a know-it-all."

COOLING OFF

Jacob was the manager of the service department at Ivers Automotive. They were the second largest dealership in town. He was lucky that he hadn't lost his job. His boss, Mr. Grant, liked him—practically everyone he met did. He was quick to laugh, respectful, industrious, and a team player. If you needed a shift picked up, or a couple of extra hours on the clock, he was your man. He'd had a drinking problem, but in the car business, that was almost a prerequisite as long as you showed up.

"You've really pulled it together Jacob, these numbers are impressive— not to mention, you helped Ivers' daughter and she gave a great report to her dad."

"It wasn't much help. She had a timing issue and—"

"That's your problem son— if someone thinks it's a big deal, let them keep on thinking it."

"I was gonna say, that without me she would've been sunk."

"There you go— and that other issue, we can't have our top man on leave."

"Yes, sir. I took care of it. My wife and I were having some issues and my coping skills were…well, not coping. But it's better now and won't trouble us again."

"Good job, Jacob. Adjustments— the carburetor of our lives sometimes needs to come online and get the, uh…that's a shitty metaphor isn't it?"

"Yes, sir."

"Good." He turned to walk away. "—You keep it up now."

"Mr. Grant, I'm sorry for uh, you know…"

"Telling me to fuck off?"

"Yeah, that."

"You weren't the last one to tell me that, as a matter of fact, my wife— just this morning, expressed that same sentiment." He squeezed Jacob's shoulder and walked back to sales.

Jacob cruised into the break room. He poured a cup of lukewarm coffee into a Styrofoam cup and lit a cigarette.

This cold shit wouldn't stand on James' watch. He had a god-damn thermometer checking the temperature of his brew. 180 degrees. Fucking Folgers, are you kidding me? I could understand if it was some special roast, but store bought? It's obsessive, man. That's the difference between him and me— I don't think about drinking that much. I'm not obsessive like those guys, it's not on me like it's on them.

His likeness— Employee of the Month, looked down from a row of Ivers luminaries.

"Are you thinking about drinking, Champ?"

He played both parts.

"Not me, buddy, I'm not thinking about drinking. I couldn't give a fuck— working better, playing better. I'm thinking about Krys."

"Me too, partner."

Yeah, I know we got our issues, but I've never loved anybody like I love her. I just need to get off that couch— what'd James say… getting my ass back in the big bed? That's right. That's what I need— a little pillow time.

BROTHER JOSEPH, SISTER EMILY

Connie woke to the sound of soft cries. Emily's bed was empty. The bathroom door cracked open— a weak sliver of light split the room. She lay silent, hoping the sobbing would stop. *Christ, the twin bed was bad enough but now this— roommate drama. Regina is such a fucking bitch.* The cries continued. She rose and knocked on the bathroom door. "Are you okay?" No answer. "Emily?"

There was a suspended silence and then more muffled tears. She gently pushed open the door— "Emily?"

"I'm okay, sorry— I'm trying to get my shirt on."

Emily was in a state of undress— slippers on her feet, bare legs, large white panties. If there was a patch of flesh that wasn't bruised, scarred, or tattooed, Connie didn't see it. Emily was struggling with a t-shirt— her left arm unresponsive, hanging by her side. There were burn scars on her back, shoulder, and neck. Connie assumed that whatever happened, it had also caused the loss of her eye.

"Let me help you—" Connie was gentler than one might imagine and maybe it was the absence of her daughters— an instinct unsatisfied needing to be addressed, or a spark of basic human kindness, but she was tender with her touch. "—Do you do this every day? It's ridiculous to wear something like this when you can't lift your arm."

"I didn't have anything else to wear. The shirt I had on was dirty."

"Where's your clothes?"

"I don't have any. Regina gave me that bag but most of them are too small."

"Oh, you were homeless? You're not part of that gang underneath the 73, are you? I heard you guys caught the whole goddamn freeway on fire— it seemed crazy to me, you lived there for god's sake, and you burned it down?"

"I wasn't homeless. My boyfriend did this."

"He took your clothes?"

"He burned them."

"What about your family— don't you have one?"

"I do but, I haven't talked to them in years."

Connie washed her hands in the sink. "—I guess when you live like that, they stay away."

"Not my dad, he had me followed— a private investigator, flyers, tip sheets, I had to leave here to get away."

"Here?"

"Ocean Park. I was born here. My parents still live in the same house— I can see it from the rec-yard."

"The rec-yard, here? That looks over West Ridge."

"That's where I was born. I lived in the upper estates— Snobville."

"I live in East Ridge."

"I remember when they built that track. You said you had two daughters— did they go to Henry?"

"No." Connie came from on high. "They went to the Crane Academy. I wouldn't think of sending them to a public school."

"I went to Crane. I would've preferred public." Emily walked out of the bathroom and retrieved a long-sleeved shirt from her bed. "I hate to bug, but could you help me with these buttons?"

At breakfast, the clients were told of that day's special event— an interview meeting, in conversation style. The guests were Father Joseph Cotton, a Jesuit from the University, and a psychologist, Dr. Carol Segar-Ward. There was a poster with photos pinned to the community board.

Carol Ward, oh my God— we were friends in college. I can't believe it; 'Ward of the State,' a psychologist. We used to live together— a cute little place over a bookstore near campus. Oh my God, they hated us. Carol couldn't handle her liquor— our place was trashed on the regular and she was known for the continuous black eye. The last time I saw her, she was naked and being stuffed into a patrol car. We lost contact after that, but I heard the gossip— suicide attempt, failed marriage, sanitarium lock-ups— the works.

Connie studied the flyer.

She looks great. If she's done all they said, it definitely didn't do her any harm.

She was excited to see her old friend and then she remembered she wasn't here on her own account. She was embarrassed. Maybe she could get out of attending— tell Regina that she wasn't feeling well.

Yeah, as if she'd cut me some slack. I'll sit in the back.

"Connie?"

She turned around.

"It *is* you. Oh my God, it's me, Carol— Carol Ward."

"Carol what a pleasure." Connie held her right arm to her side, the plastic Bayside bracelet hidden in the folds of her sweats. "I thought that was you."

"I can't believe it. I thought about looking you up— tell me true, Robert Hedge, you married Hedge?"

"Yeah, he was—"

"Dreamy. I remember when you guys hooked up at Dean's house." She lowered her voice, an old college conspirator. "—you were so fucked up."

"Carol!"

"Come on, don't be such a prude. Remember, what'd you call our apartment?"

"Don't do it."

"The Pussy Palace! Ha!"

"Aren't you here with a priest?"

"Yeah, but he's wearing the smock, honey— not me. I'm sober, not dead."

"You're sober?"

"Of course— twenty-two years last August. Do you think I'd be standing here if I wasn't?"

"Not really. I heard some things after you left."

"Probably not the half of it— I've done things that no woman should ever admit to. Hey, speaking of things, I was talking to Cindy Mulligan— remember her? She said you got tazed at Antonio's! Oh my God!"

"It's not funny."

"No, it's not, but it can be, if you stay sober."

"I don't have a drinking problem, Carol."

"Neither did I."

Father Joseph was an alcoholic— fifteen drunk drivings, and a suspension for insubordination. He was sober forty-seven years— *I was a baby when he put down the bottle. I wonder why he drank. All I hear around here is pray and pray and more pray. Why the hell should I do it, if it didn't do him any good.*

"Did you ask God to strike you sober? I mean, if anyone had the direct pipeline to the All Mighty it'd be one of you, right?"

The audience laughed.

"I actually did. I implored God many times, and my prayers, or my entreaties, went unanswered."

"Did you question your belief?"

"Of course— who doesn't, especially when we go through trials; the death of a loved one, a disease bestowed upon a person who we see as innocent, the horror of war, the mental illness inherent in man? I'm being a touch dramatic here, but what do you expect when you cross alcoholism with religion? I'd devoted my life to God. I expected to be rewarded for my service."

"I'm not of your faith, but that sounds like blasphemy."

Father Joseph laughed. "You don't get suspended for sleeping in church."

"So, what did you do?"

"I felt like I was alone. It's written— not in the Bible, but in a secular work, *'in a real dark night of the soul it's always three o'clock in the morning, day after day.'* And how true that is for the alcoholic— the disease of loneliness. I was waiting for a miracle— a physical manifestation from a detached God. It didn't come. But what arrived— in that place of desolation was a thought, and again with the dramatics… it was a voice from beyond me, and it said, *'He is not a God of ink and paper; He is a God of action and deed— the manifestation of the Word.'* God would do nothing for me that I was not willing to do for myself."

"So, again, Father Joe, what did you do?"

"I finished my bottle." The audience laughed. "Look, I wasn't going to let good scotch go to waste. I might've been broken, but I wasn't an idiot."

"Seriously?"

He stared at her, a wry grin on his face that broke into a smile. "The next morning, I woke a new man. I knew where the twelve-step meetings were and I went there. But I didn't walk into that group as a leader— a priest standing at the head of the room. I walked in as a novice— as I remain today. I swept floors, cleaned ashtrays, and I took those steps. I admitted I had been without power— a crushing blow for someone who supposedly knew God. I saw the insanity— thinking that I could do this without my fellows, and I said a devotion to my new

understanding of Our Lord. I realized I had begged with my faith—
Father please, father please, father please. I was like Oliver holding out
my plate. I stopped begging, and I gave."

"Do you believe God placed that thought?"

"I don't know. I know some that would— a miracle if you will that
got that old drunk Father Joe to put down the bottle, but I'm not so
sure… "

"But surely it was your faith… "

"Faith in myself to get off my ass and put in the work? Faith in the
union of man and God, a team working together? Hope that if I poked
him enough times he'd get off his ass and do something?"

"I can see why you were suspended."

"I can't give you that answer. All I know is that I was once blind
and now I see."

He sat quietly for a moment and Carol honored that pause. The air
in the room became stilled, he leaned forward, and took a breath.

"A woman came into the program at the same time as me. She was
an atheist. She sought me for counsel, but there was nothing I could give
her other than friendship. The steps were written as they are. I couldn't
change them. But she took the steps without God— confessed her
shortcomings, righted her wrongs, and became a servant to those who
needed her. Do you know how many years of sobriety she has— this
godless heathen?"

"Zero?"

"Not at all. She has forty-seven beautiful years of recovery."

The audience applauded.

"But wait, what of a spiritual awakening— isn't that a must?"

"Nietzsche said that—"

"Nietzsche? The 'God is dead' Nietzsche? Are you kidding me?"

"Yes, that Nietzsche. As you know that quote was more about the
loss of morals— Martin Luther King Jr. said similar; 'Now we have
guided missiles and mis-guided men.' But I'm referring to his take on

the Kingdom of God, that it's not a place in heaven, but a condition of heart. I believe that if your heart never becomes a kingdom of love and acceptance, then you were never awake. I've never seen a white flash, heard a voice booming from a burning bush, or had a heavenly apparition appear before me, but I have seen God in my fellow's eyes."

"One last question before we leave— and thank you for your insights. Is a belief in God necessary to work these steps?"

"You mean the steps that say God four times out of twelve, with an implied *Him*?" The audience laughed. "Well, some would have you believe so, but our founder, the man who outlined this program wrote, 'you don't have to believe in God, you just have to *disclaim* that you are God.'"

It was a good talk— honestly, better than I thought. Maybe they'll let us coast for the rest of the day— that was a lot of information to digest. I wonder if the church knows he's talking like that.

Carol caught up to her in the snack line.

"Did you enjoy it?"

"It was interesting. Do you work for the church?"

"Heavens no. I'm friends with Joe. We thought a program like this might benefit those new in recovery."

"Well, I can tell you this— it was a hell of a lot better than most of our groups."

"That's what we thought. We've gone to a few treatment centers and we're getting good feedback— hey, I talked to Dr. Plummer."

"I don't know who that is."

"He runs the facility— that's him with the beard, talking to Father Joe. He said that he thought it might be beneficial if you went out with me tonight. I got you a pass!"

"To leave?"

"A few hours with me—"

"Let me get my sweater and change these clothes— I'm out in five."

"Not now, silly! Tonight. I'll be back at 6:30 to pick you up. It'll be a blast."

LADIES NIGHT

Connie's bare face told the tale of every minute she'd spent in the world, and she'd surrendered her cash and credit cards on admittance, but she was dressed, and in the lobby, at 6:15— signed pass in hand.

I love seeing Regina without power. I bet she would've given anything to deny me. Thank God, for Dr. Plummer— hey, maybe prayer does work. I asked Baby Jesus to get that bitch off my back and look what happened— poof! I'm heading out, and she's on the sidelines— hopefully, fingers deep in some retard's bedpan. I think we'll get a bite at that pop-up place next to the theatre and then grab a couple glasses of wine at D'Angelo's. I sure hope Carol doesn't stop me from enjoying my evening. I don't care if she doesn't, why should she care if I do?

Carol arrived on time, dressed in a pair of sweats and tennis shoes. "You ready to go?"

"I've been ready since this morning. What were you thinking, the pop-ups downtown?"

"The pop-ups?" She clicked the alarm on a late model sedan. "— We're going to the meeting at the park and then, if we get time, we'll hit the diner with the gang."

"I thought we were going out."

"And you dressed like that? Ha!" Connie was crushed. She had nothing decent to wear. "I'm teasing— they're not going to let you out of Bayside for dinner with a friend. Are you kidding? You're going to a meeting with your sponsor."

"You're not my sponsor."

"I am now. I'm vouching for you— you're skipping out on that tasty Bayside chicken dinner extravaganza."

Connie weighed her options —this, or that— *definitely not that.*

"Of course, if you'd like to go back I could swing around and drop you off."

Connie gazed at open country and took a breath of air that didn't smell of disinfectant, hand sanitizer, and desperation— "No, this is great, Carol. Thanks."

Carol was pretty good behind the wheel— no excessive lane changing, tail-gating, or driving too slow. She did get a touch tiffed about me reaching over and employing the horn, but if I hadn't acted she could've killed that kid. What's with these people that express displeasure instead of gratitude? Robert's the same way. I'm not looking for a big 'thank you, Connie' but you don't expect to be yelled at for helping out.

They parked in the back lot, Carol's front bumper kissing a pole that held a No Parking sign.

"So, what happened that night, after the police took you away?"

"What do you mean what happened?"

"I mean, I heard all the stories, Carol, but it was like you disappeared."

"I went to treatment."

"Did the court send you?"

"Yeah, but it's not that simple. When I was locked up I threatened to kill myself. I don't remember saying it, but knowing what I know

now it sounds on the money. I was all screwed up over Kyle— you remember him, the bartender at Duke's. My grades were in the crapper, and I was basically over it— tired of living."

"But you never talked like that. You were fun— always up. I can see them being tiffed about the alcohol thing but wanting to die?"

"The alcohol kept me alive. You never know what lies beneath the smile. Do you remember that boy from freshman year?"

"I think I know who you're talking about."

"He had it all. He was dating that Linda Dixon— honor roll, tennis star."

"He hung himself."

"That's right— did you call that?"

"No. I was as shocked as everyone else."

"Me too, but I understood where he came from."

"I don't want to burst your bubble, Ward, but you weren't showing that kind of promise."

"No, but I was showing a disconnection, a self-hate, and a life on the edge."

"I didn't think you were any worse than the rest of us."

"You're making this too easy, Connie. The rest of us? Barry?"

"He's gone, you know that. He got in that wreck junior year— him and his fiancée."

"Mark?"

"I see where you're going with this— his arrest wasn't for alcohol. He assaulted his mother for Christ's sake."

"Alcohol related— I've spoken to him. He's living in Hardy. Has six years clean under his belt."

"Okay, I'll play. How about Dean?"

"He's doing great— owns his own business and is happily married."

"There it is."

"There's three more, Connie. Carol, once a drunk, now sober twenty-two years and… "

"Really, you're going to include me and Robert?"

"You were part of that little gang— those Jefferson High molecules that banded together. Robert— happily married? The last I checked, his wife assaulted him and now she's in rehab. And then there's Connie— how many arrests is this now, four?"

"Three."

"Great. Three arrests, in rehab, and a marriage on the ropes. So, out of six people— five of us are suffering from one tendril of the disease or another."

"I didn't come out here to be brow-beaten by you. Things are hard— Robert and I were having some relationship issues and the pressure got to me. If you're going to continue, I'd rather you take me back."

"You're right. I apologize... I've always liked you, Connie. I looked up to you. I'll keep this with me.

"They put me on a 5150— a hold for saying I was going to kill myself. While I was there I spoke to a counselor. I thought I was playing it straight— saying the things she wanted to hear, but she ended up doubling the hold— 5250."

"They have that?"

"Yes they do. I ended up agreeing to go to an out-of-state treatment center. I got ninety days, worked on some issues, was in the best shape of my life and I coined out. I got a job doing tables at a local restaurant, and I signed up for school. Four months later I picked up a drink. It was so innocent— after work, a couple of us hanging around and they offered me a beer. I don't even like beer, but I reached out and grabbed one without thinking. One beer, that was it. I didn't explode or run naked through the street, the police weren't involved, it was no big deal. I went home and went to bed. A week later I drank again. And then I continued to drink— on and off, for about a year. Your hats were off to me, as they say. I remained fairly happy, well adjusted, and basically normal. My counselor said that the illness picks up where it leaves off, but not for me. It was a slow progression to that place that you'd witnessed... but then it kept going. I had no idea how low I could sink. I'm not sure when my last drink was, but I know what the morning of my first day sober looked like. It was August eighth. I woke up in an unfamiliar bed next to a very unattractive, unfamiliar man. I retrieved my clothes. My bra was torn, my panties and my pants were soaked with urine and hanging like shame-filled flags on the bedposts. I walked out to a car that I barely recognized— dents, torn fender, the interior littered with trash and empty bottles. I was on empty. I wondered how I was going to get home and then I realized that I'd lost my place. I'd been crashing where I could, using my body as rent money. I called my parents from a payphone. They hung up. I called again— the first word out of my mouth was please, the second, help. I hitch-hiked to a hotel. The rehab picked me up. I was a year sober before my parents talked to me again."

She paused for a moment, broke eye contact with Connie, and glanced in the side-view mirror. People were leaving the hall, cars pulling out of the lot—"Shit, is the meeting over, what are they doing?"

A year... her family didn't speak to her for a year. I can't imagine Robert and the girls doing that to me. Carol was awful— really put them through it. I was nothing compared to her. She was insane for Christ's sake. I was just unruly— okay, maybe a bit demanding and a trifle bossy, but not a year's worth. You can't blame her family for turning away.

Carol got out of the car and straightened her outfit. Connie followed, her pace slow.

She's a sad tale— it looks like a happy ending, but it sure doesn't feel like one.

Connie hung back while Carol said hello to a few old friends. She didn't feel like being introduced. She wanted to go back to Bayside.

The food's not as bad as she made it out to be—sure, it's no chef's treat, but you wouldn't feel depressed after eating it. If I have to listen to one more of these sob stories, I'll be the one they lock up as insane.

She was standing by the side door when Carol approached. "I just want to say 'hi' to one more— come on. I promise we'll leave right after this."

She followed Carol into the kitchen. James, the coffeemaker, was cleaning up. His young friend Jacob was bagging trash. James had been sober forever— thirty years, but Jacob was new. She forced a smile as she took James' hand, but when they made eye contact, she could tell he sensed her effort. She couldn't mask the sadness.

"You been around a while, Connie?"

"No." She flashed her Bayside bracelet.

"Rehab." He smiled. "Here's to new beginnings. If you come back, make sure you say hello." He nodded toward Jacob. "—My apprentice needs another set of eyes on him and you look like a woman in charge."

"Being in charge seems to have been lost on me, but if I ever do come back I'll make sure to say hello. Thank you. I'll meet you outside, Carol."

Five out of six. It seems a bit exaggerated. There were a couple thousand people at that school— the odds have got to be much lower than that— crazy pyscho-babble.

"Connie?" The mother of one of her daughter's friends was standing on the path. "It's good to see you, here."

She kept walking— *I'm pretty sure that bitch went to Carver.*

DIFFERENT VOICES

As the days passed, a stream of speakers visited the hall. Each member had worked the twelve steps in their own way. Each voice was as different as a snowflake in the field. "Within the framework of the principles," their founder had said. "—the ways were apparently legion."

*****

"And isn't this a glorious night to be sober and praising God in all his wisdom? It wasn't always so, my friends. I had turned my back on everything I believed in, and the bottle had become my higher power. I went from being on my knees in church to praying before the porcelain bowl. And I will tell you this, the last thing my God wanted to see was this beautiful big black ass, pointed up at the heavens, as I blasphemed into that toilet." Winnie B— sober 42 years.

*****

"I thought I'd walked into a cult. God grant me this, God grant me that. I didn't come in here for all this shit. I was looking for a consultation and a three-day follow up. I figured it was only a matter of time before they had me on a street corner, passing out pamphlets— Jeez was I wrong." Mark M— sober 10 years.

*****

"They said they'd turned their will and their life over to the care of God. Now I don't know about you, but I'd been told since my very first crush— Tommy Winslow, in third grade, that there was a special place in hell for nasty little boys like me. The thought of a loving God was a concept so foreign, so difficult. I had to use the group as my higher power... I used you." Rickie S— sober 2 years.

*****

"I don't know if there is or isn't a God, but if there were, I don't believe, as a human, that I would have the capacity to see it. I can't see wind, but I can see the reaction of the trees and I can feel it against my skin. I can't see God, but I can see the power that has manifested in your lives." Pete the Professor— sober 27 years.

A woman approached Tina as she searched the hall for Albert— *mother fucker was just here, talking to some dude by the bathrooms, and now he's wandering around with these fucking people. I think he needs some sort of mental help or something. His brother was the same way. It's like they're not in their right minds.*

"Do you need help?"

"No, I've got a few signatures left and I'm done."

"I'm Dotty."

"I'm looking for my Beto."

"Is he on the program?"

"Look lady, I appreciate you trying to minister or whatever the fuck you're doing but— there he is."

Tina walked away as if the woman never existed.

"Where were you? I can't believe you fucking left me there— some old bitch tried to convert me."

Albert handed her a book. "I bought this from the court-card lady."

"Why are you giving it to me? I'm not reading that shit." She handed it back.

"I thought you might want to see what they're doing here."

"I know what they're doing— a room full of fools listening to each other brag about what bad-asses they are. That fucking old lady yesterday, I'd like to take her on a ride."

"I don't hear too much bragging."

"What about that fucking *chavalo* the other day— two gallons of booze a day my ass— king of Bolivia, he looked like that punk you beat on Sunset. Remember that *puto*— crying like a little girl."

Albert remembered him. He was one of the faces that he was struggling to forget. The alcohol had put distance between him and his past, but now that he hadn't drank, his past was stepping up. "You haven't heard anything useful?"

"Sure, I heard that old man say he could've signed his own card."

POP

Part of Bayside's recovery program was intensive counseling. The clients were expected to attend groups, and twice weekly speak to a therapist. It was Connie's turn in the chair.

"Are you still having difficulties with the staff, Connie?"

"Why don't you just say 'Regina', Patty? You know that bitch hates me. I can't believe you guys let crap like that go on here— gestapo, that's what it is. You give someone a little power and they run wild— especially people like her."

"What kind of people is she?"

"You know what I'm talking about— her people, drug addicts that get cleaned up and have nothing else. They come to places like this and try to be big shots."

"I'm pretty sure that Regina graduated from a very reputable school."

"Are you sticking up for her?"

"No, I just wanted you to have as much information as possible. You seem to me to be a woman that would want to have all the facts before you formed an opinion."

"I try to be."

"Is there anyone else you're troubled with— relationships that you might want to discuss?"

"I haven't been able to speak with my girls. I'm not sure what Robert is up to— if he thinks he's going to divorce me, he'll be sorry. I'll have him in a fucking tent on the sidewalk. Encouraging my children to not speak with me is crossing the line."

"How did you find out he was doing that?"

"Did you know?"

"Excuse me?"

"You just asked me how I found out— what information do you have on it, Patty? I'd like to see your sheet."

"I'm sorry, Connie. I should have been clearer. I have no information of that sort. They signed up for the family afterward program, but I haven't spoken to any of them."

"Well, I have— not the girls, but Robert. He said they were embarrassed of me and he couldn't force them to call— embarrassed, what a load of shit. He *was* right on his inability to extend force, though. I'm surprised he had the power to dial."

"Embarrassed… that's an interesting word."

"How so?"

"What if we were to expand on that, hypothetically? Have they ever been embarrassed of you before?"

"Hypothetically?"

"It can be a helpful exercise. I wouldn't attempt it with our average guest, but I think with your intuition, it might be very helpful."

"Hypothetically?" She took a deep breath and closed her eyes. She couldn't imagine either Britney or Bridget being embarrassed of her, but there was a memory that flittered on the edge of consciousness…

I'd just returned from a girl's day out. Bridget needed a ride to her friends and Robert was late getting home. I offered to take her— it was practically a fight to get her in the car. She was crying about not having a ride, and then not wanting to go. On the way over, she complained about my driving— teens, they act as if they understand the rules of the road, and yet, they've never been behind a wheel. There was one moment that the arguing got so bad— I was so distracted, that we almost had an accident. We could've killed someone. When we finally arrived, Bridget practically jumped from the car. There was no 'I love you,' no 'thank you,' and then I saw Cheryl— the girl's mother. I waved to her— wanted to say hello, but she grabbed Bridget and went inside. I sat in the car for a moment, and then I checked my make-up in the mirror. One of my lashes was hanging down, and my face was blotchy and red— I reeked of wine. I was a mess— a drunk, a fucking sot.

"Connie, I asked if they've ever been embarrassed of you before?"

"Yes… yes they have."

"They've been embarrassed by you?"

"Yes, I said, yes."

"Would you like to expand on that?"

It was as if cards were being flashed before her— pictures of her life slapped onto the consciousness of the moment— her daughters, her husband, her mother, her friends, all of them flashing before her, all of them wearing that same mask of disgust on their faces. She stared blankly at Patty as the bile of awakening gathered in her throat— "You want me to expand on that? Yeah, I'll fucking expand on that— fuck, fuck, fuck, fuck, fuck!"

She pounded the arms of the chair as she broke, unmanageable tears running down her face, staining her blouse with acceptance and disgust.

Patty let her cry.

THE BEAUTY SHOP

A worn Rapunzel blanket covered a graveyard of dolls— Kiggles, Mr. Skrunchy, and the large blue dragon named Burt lorded over the denizens of C.C.'s room. Jacob had built a beauty shop in the center of her pink shag rug— two chairs on either side of a small table adorned with brilliantly colored crayon scribbles and her mother's best brush— an item that was not allowed outside the dressing area in her parent's room. Jacob wore an assortment of hair ties on his wrist. His voice was affectedly flamboyant.

"Oh my God. Your hair is atrocious. Look at this mess. I'm surprised you don't have a family of rats living in there... you know, the other day I did your mother's hair."

"You did not."

"Yes, I did, and do you want to know what I found— beside the fact that she's not a real blonde?"

"Daddy!"

Krystal hovered by the door— a slight smile on her face, unconcerned that her boar bristle hairbrush was off-premises and in the hands of an unlicensed stylist.

"I found a wart."

"You did not!"

"I did— large and puffy and tinged an evil shade of green. I think she might be a witch."

"You're terrible!"

"I am not. I'm a beauty professional skilled in the disciplines of hair, make-up, and witch hunting."

"Are you serious?"

"Deadly."

"Time-out, dad."

Jacob checked his watch. He picked up the brush— hopefully Krys hadn't missed it.

"Dad?"

He resumed his normal speaking voice. "Look Ceace, I'm not saying that she is or isn't a witch, but common table salt— strategically placed on a kitchen counter or table, could cause her enough discomfort to be a telltale sign if she was a spawn of the devil."

"Spawn?"

"A witch." He bent down and kissed her goodbye. "—Gotta go!"

THE PROSPECT

He was out of pomade— the last dab swept from the edges of the can.

Tina was supposed to pick some up, but like everything else, it hadn't materialized. It's okay. Any less and I'd wear a net, but I'm good for the evening— a fine hold.

His pants had a sharp crease, the iron still hot. His t-shirt tucked in, the top button of his green checked flannel secured. The bluebird perched on his neck, peeked over his collar. He was solid.

"Albert, I need to get in there." Her voice carrying through the closed bathroom door.

"What you need to do is get ready." He checked himself once more, avoiding his eyes. Tina was waiting outside.

"Did you shave? Who are you getting fixed up for?"

"The meeting— go on, get dressed."

She walked into the bathroom, pulled up her skirt and sat down. "Baby, I'm done. I turned my card in today."

"Good. Now get dressed."

"I'm not going to that fucking meeting— God-damn-it, Beto. You didn't buy paper. I told you we were out."

"I'd tell you to wipe yourself with pomade, but we're out of that too, huh."

"I forgot." She wiped with her panties and dropped them on the floor. "—let's go to Jessie's."

He checked his hair once more. "Not tonight."

"You're taking this too far." She rubbed up against him, put her hand on his crotch. "—come on, we'll get a couple 40s, you can fuck me in the car."

He pushed her away. "I'm gonna go."

"I liked you better when you were drinking— this new Beto, the good boy, isn't good for me."

There was a difference to the hall. He could feel it when he pulled in. The lot was full like always, but there was a solemn air, it resembled a funeral— suits, dresses, ties, and serious looks— *maybe somebody died.* He found a spot in the back— the row of No Parking signs, normally blocked by cars, were empty. A man approached him. He was wearing a dark blue suit— white shirt, red tie.

"We try to follow the rules around here."

"The lot was full, *vato.*" Albert stiffened his right leg and grabbed his knee with his hand. "—somebody jammed up the wheelchair spot, ey."

"Oh, I'll look into it."

"Hey, this is twelve-step, right— somebody die?"

"It's a serious illness— people die on a daily basis. Are you new?"

"No— I'm a veteran."

There was a greeting line at the door— a row of suits and ties and dresses and white teeth and eager hands. The atmosphere felt stiff but there were smiles— *it's like that fucking* Stepford Wives *thing, a bunch of robots. I bet if I spilt coffee on one of them, they'd sizzle.* He didn't see any familiar faces as he weaved through the crowd. There was no-one sitting, but the chairs were occupied by paper or keys, claimed by someone. He took a seat on the aisle— his usual row in the back. He was immediately accosted by two clean-shaven young men in business attire. They were no-nonsense.

"Good evening, Andy Bartlow, alcoholic. That seat is saved."

"Yeah, thanks, man. I appreciate it." Albert remained seated.

"I mean, that's my seat."

"You weren't sitting in it. Get that one."

Andy's companion spoke up. "He's been sitting in it for fifteen years."

"Sounds like it's time for your boss to move, ey?"

Andy wasn't sure what to do. He considered himself a voice of authority in the group. "We earn our seats here."

"I said, fuck off, fool."

Andy and his companion walked away, but their voices remained— "I don't worry about guys like that. He's not going to stay sober. An alcoholic of our type knows when he's licked— there's a humility about us. I've seen it…"

Albert lost track of Andy's voice as the seats filled. There was a general expression of mild disgust as the surrounding attendees saw Albert already settled.

They read the usual readings and then a stern man— his audience smile contained to just his mouth, stepped to the lectern. He looked like an older version of boss Andy.

"Good evening. My name is Charles White, and I am a fully recovered alcoholic."

The group chorus was militant. "—Good evening, Charles!"

"I've been sober thirty-eight years. I have a sponsor that has a sponsor, and they both know that I am their sponsee. I have a home group, and I sponsor many men. You'll notice that I did not say I sponsor men and women. Around here, the men stick with the men, and the women stick with the women."

Albert thought Charles was having a go at them. He laughed and smiled at the woman sitting near. She ignored him.

"I was taught that you will wear clothing that shows your respect to the program. Men, suits and ties; women, dresses or skirts."

This fucking vato *ain't fooling*— "*Jefe's* tripping, ey?"

Again, his neighbor paid him no mind.

The sober lecture of control continued— an axe being ground on the minds of those in attendance. "When you see these steps, you will see that they are written in order and made to be done in order. You've worked *your* program long enough. Now it's time to work 'The Program.'"

Albert was done.

His neighbor finally acknowledged him when he got to his feet— "We don't get up during the speaker."

Albert smiled at her. "Fuck you, ma'am."

With a look of disgust, she turned away.

Albert walked out of the hall and into the night. He was thirsting— the hole in his soul begging to be filled.

He walked by James, who was sitting against the trunk of his car— leather coat, a cigar in hand, a thin cloud of smoke loitering about him.

"Fuck these people."

"You leaving?"

"I don't fucking see you in there, man."

James spoke, but Albert couldn't hear him. He was somewhere else, between here and there, but closer to his past than he realized.

As Albert unlocked the door to their apartment he was telling the tale. "—Tina, that fucking place was trippy, man. You should have been there… it was like zombies had taken over and uh…" The scent of weed, burnt devotional candles, and alcohol checked him at the threshold.

She had company.

Tina was sitting in the corner chair, her right foot resting on the floor, her left leg crossed beneath her. She was wearing a pair of jean shorts cut too close for visitors. Her shirt was unbuttoned, her bra exposed. His friend Jesse and an unknown were with her. They'd been drinking.

"Look who it is. It's the good boy."

The three of them laughed. He could forgive Jessie his joke— they'd been friends for years.

"Fucking Pepsi, boy."

This unknown hadn't earned that. "Do I fucking know you, *vato*?"

"Come on, baby. That's Angel."

"Fuck you, Tina."

Angel stood up and shook his head. "—You shouldn't talk to her like that. Tina needs a good man, not a boy."

Albert was on him.

He yanked the gun from his waistband, grabbed Angel's hair, and punched him repeatedly in the face using the pistol as a hammer— the blood, alcohol heavy, fountained with each thrust. Jessie tried to flee, but Albert was between him and the door. In desperation, he sought the kitchen— the stairway to the alley. Albert fired a wild shot that shattered the press-board cabinets— the dishes chattering encased. Angel lay bleeding at his feet— unconscious.

Albert wiped his mouth with the back of his hand, a swipe of fresh blood painted across his face. He stood over Tina, rage clenched in his fist. "—You want a bad boy, Tina? You want some of this?"

Breathing heavily, he lifted his arm and stared down the barrel toward her. She pulled her legs beneath her as if they could stop his intention.

"—or maybe, you want another dead brother, ey?" He put the gun against his head, gritted his teeth— his hand squeezed the metal as if it could crush. "Fuck you. You're not worth it. Pick up your trash and get the fuck out of here."

He stepped over Angel as he tucked the blood covered gun in his waistband.

Albert drove to the Blue Fairy, parked at the curb, and watched the brown paper bags exit in the hands of the customers. He could see the beads of sweat on the bottles.

I know how those twist caps feel when you turn them in your hand— the pinch of the crumpled aluminum cutting the skin of your thumb. I know the weight of a 40, the space a pint takes in your pocket, and the taste of the wine— the thick sweet pour of Moscato, Night Train, and T-Bird. I know all those things. I can taste them and feel them and smell them in my mind, but I have no desire to do them. I feel like a sick boy trapped in a candy shop— these treats aren't for you, Beto.

In confused frustration, he left.

James had just locked up as Albert pulled in. Other than the two men, the parking lot was empty. They met in the space between their cars. James was the first to speak.

"You're back."

"I didn't know where to go, man."

"You okay?"

"No. I don't know what the fuck's wrong with me."

"I'm guessing you're not sedated."

"What the fuck does that mean— are you fucking with me?"

"No, of course not. I know that look— a human animal trying to escape itself." James held out his hand. "I'm James."

Albert hesitated and then reached for him. He put his head down and cried. James moved to hug him, but Albert pulled away, embarrassed by his emotions— broken before a stranger. He wiped his eyes with his sleeve.

"How come you weren't inside tonight? I saw you sitting on your car."

"Is that why you're so upset?"

Albert surrendered a smile. "Seriously, man. Was that twelve-step?"

"It's *their* interpretation of the program. It's not *my* thing, but some people need that."

"Why don't you need it?"

"Because I'm not a fan of following orders. I've always thought it funny— the guys that started this shit back in the 30s, they knew us pretty well. They knew we didn't like to be told what to do— no lectures, no promises to make, no one in charge. You either do it or you don't."

"And you do it?"

"It's my life. I couldn't imagine living any other way."

"But what makes you? Are you on a card?"

"Nobody makes me. How old are you, uh…"

"Albert— Beto, either way it's me. Thirty-two last week."

"Happy birthday. I got sober when you were two. If I was still on a court card, I'd be in trouble. I do this because I know what's good for me. It's a code of conduct that I try to live by— principles." James looked Albert over. When their eyes met, Albert turned away, but James caught the scared boy beneath. "Why did you come back *here*?"

"I didn't have anywhere else to go— this felt safe."

"And you haven't been drinking."

"No."

"Why not?"

"I haven't had a drink since the first time I came."

"Why not?"

"What the fuck's with you, man?"

"Answer me. It's a simple question."

"Because I don't want to fucking do it anymore. I take a drink and the bottle owns me— I'm a fucking bitch to that sauce, standing behind it like a man without heart. I don't want that life. It doesn't work for me. I bought a bottle— ah, fucking Tina bought me a 40 after our first time, but I didn't drink it. I was gonna, but it didn't feel the same."

"As if the power was out of it?"

"Yeah, I guess, something like that. Like before, the bottle was real heavy. It used to call to me. It doesn't anymore, but I'm not right without it. I'm fucking *loco*, man."

"Hold up, so you know the booze doesn't work anymore, and you feel crazy, or insane if you will, without it, and you came here— thinking that something might help you."

"Yeah… that sounds right."

"Let me ask you something— are you willing to try *this* way of life?"

"I don't want to feel like this anymore, and I won't drink again. I guess I'd do what it takes."

"Well, you made that easy."

"What?"

"You just took the first three steps."

"I did?"

"Yeah, and most people take forever to do what you just— "

"Will you pray for me?"

I was uncomfortable but I knew he needed it and it didn't hurt me. I wasn't a hypocrite; it was what he believed and I honored him.

James put his arm around Albert's shoulders. "I'll pray with you. God, if you can hear us, believe that we want to serve you. Guide our hands. Bless your son Albert."

Albert lifted his shirt and held the gun out to James. For the first time, James noticed the blood on his new friend.

"It looks like it's time for damage assessment. Are the police looking for you?"

"You mean, did somebody call? I doubt it. We're not white, man."

"I'll forgive your racist insensitivities. Did you kill anyone?"

"Tonight?" Albert held a straight serious look. He jokingly put James in check. "No, I beat this fucking mouthy fool for shooting off, but he's no-one. He was breathing when I left— probably fucking my girlfriend."

"Excellent— not the fucking part, the breathing. Do you have a place to stay? Can you go home?"

"I guess. I don't know if Tina split, but I told her to get out."

"You can stay with us if you like— my wife and me. Give it the night to cool off. We've got an extra room— my daughter is away."

"*La Neta*?" James didn't understand the question. "You for real, man?"

"Two conditions... make that three. One: you wash that fucking blood off your hands. Two: you don't tell anybody you saw me praying. And three: lose the gun."

THE SLEEPOVER

"I'm assuming we have a visitor." Sarah pushed James' hand away from her teacup. "—let it steep. You might know coffee, but the Earl Grey is out of your jurisdiction." She was dressed for work. James was in pajamas, an unlit cigar in his hand.

He poked the cup with his smoke. "—Every time I see you sipping that shit I question your alcoholism."

"Go easy, baby. I once killed a man for a brick of chamomile."

A bedroom door opened down the hallway— heavy steps traversed a polished cement floor.

"By the way, I made a new friend last night."

Albert walked into the kitchen, his sleeves were rolled up and his flannel buttoned down. The bloodstains of the evening were hidden from view.

"May I introduce young Albert?"

"Good morning, ma'am."

James placed his hands on Sarah's hips and turned her toward their guest. "—Strike one, Beto! You never call a woman who looks like this 'ma'am.'"

Sarah offered Albert her hand. "I'm assuming this falls under the thirty-day rule. How long have you been sober, Albert?"

"Twenty-seven days— twenty-eight, today."

"Then I forgive you. There's coffee in the pot, and if James will spare you any of his Cap'n Crunch, it's in the cupboard." She kissed her husband and grabbed her bag. "—I got to go, baby. I'll see you tonight."

Albert took a seat at the table. James set a coffee before him.

"She lets you smoke that in the house?"

"Only when I want to get my ass kicked. How are you doing?"

"I slept good— that bed is something else, eh? I folded the blankets and the sheets." He pushed at his coffee but didn't drink. "I feel strange— like guilty or something. I mean, he fucking deserved it, but I feel sick about it. I never felt this way before."

"I assume you're talking about your friend?"

"I don't know him. He must've come with Jessie, he's not from the neighborhood— Angel, that's his name."

"Do you want to talk about it?"

"We can. Do you want to smoke that?"

"Always—." James was up, lit, and walking toward the sliding glass door— a trail of guilty smoke weaving its way through the living room.

They sat on the balcony, a view of the ocean and the point in the distance. The sound of the waves breaking on the beach swam beneath Albert's story…

"—And then I just split, I thought about drinking but, it was strange man, like I couldn't even if I wanted to, and then I ran into you."

"That's why I asked you if it had power. I enjoy knowing I'm not alone. When I was about ninety days in, I got in a fight with my ex-wife. I was obsessed with her— restraining orders, the whole thing."

"You had papers served?"

"You haven't?" James played with his lighter. "Hey, the way I see it, if they didn't have to restrain you, you didn't really love 'em."

"*Oralé!*"

"I prove my devotion… Just don't go saying shit like that in the meetings. There are some real sensitive drunks around here. They don't think it's funny. Anyway, when she took off, I was devastated. I went to the liquor store, and I bought a bottle of vodka."

"Ah, *el jefe*."

"It was Popov $1.99. I bought it, but it didn't feel the same, almost as if it was nothing— a non-entity. I'd normally take the cap off the moment I walked from the store, but not that time. I kept that bottle with me for hours— didn't drink it, and then I poured the vodka in the toilet and tossed the bottle in the trash. I kinda wish I would've kept the empty. It would've been cool to say that this bottle was proof of change."

"I wish you would've, man. It feels good to know you think like me. I thought I was crazy."

"I'm not the only one. They say that when you come to twelve-step, you can meet strangers and reminisce— a room full of crazies, brothers and sisters that've shared your past and think like you do."

James took a long hit of his smoke. As he exhaled, the sea breeze scattered the cloud. "I remember this old guy— Fast Eddie. He was great— lost a lung, kept smoking, lost his money, kept gambling. Not an outstanding role model, but he was sober a long time and always had something positive to say. Anyway, one day as I was sweeping up, he came over to me and said, I don't know about these other people, but you and I, we're the real thing. I was stoked, thinking that I belonged, and then the next week I overheard him talking to someone else. I don't know about these other people, he said, but you and I are the real thing."

"Ha! My *tío* Bobby was like that— always pulling someone aside, whispering something that he just whispered to ten other dudes. Maybe he was a drunk… no, not maybe. He always had a bottle in his hand."

"Good for him. I like drunks— sober drunks most of all. We're good people when we're heading in the right direction."

"So, what should I do?"

"With what?"

"With going on— you said I did the first three, now what?"

James took another hit of his cigar. "I can only tell you what they told me. When I was new, the old-timers stressed physical sobriety— putting distance between myself and that last drink. You said you've been going to meetings— keep it up. I'd like you to get a commitment at the hall, a little job sweeping floors or wiping down tables."

"Does it pay?"

"Millions over time, but if you're looking for a paycheck for doing the right thing— paying your debt to society, being of service, you're talking to the wrong guy."

"Okay, I hear you, but what about today? It's only morning."

"Do you read?"

"I read the labels on the bottle."

"Excellent, literacy is a plus, but not a requirement. Come with me—" He led Albert into the house, and gave him a small book. "—this is a daily devotional of how our founder saw things. It's a good place to start."

"My *tita* used to read one— every morning."

"Your teacher?"

"My grandmother— *Ay Cabrón!* I'm gonna have to wipe some white off you."

"I look forward to it— you can start with my ass. Did you like this... tita?"

"I'm here because of her. She was the best person I've ever known."

"Then think of her when you read it. Your head is probably full of old ideas— let's fill it with new ones."

They read the page of the day— it asked them to be on the lookout for selfishness and self-seeking motives.

"I think that's a great start. If you come across something that's hard to understand, call me and we'll go over it. If you come across something cool, share it with me. Don't assume I've seen something or that I'm not willing to learn. The ripe fruit rots on the vine. I need to stay green just like you do."

James walked Albert to his car. "—Look, buddy. I know I've been pumping you full of all sorts of advice, and I'm sorry about that, but I can't be with you twenty-four/seven, so you have to know how to think on your own. When you get home, I'd suggest cleaning your house. Throw out any booze that's lying around— weed, pills, whatever. If you don't want to dump it, give it to a neighbor— preferably an adult knowledgeable in recreational activities. I know you said the power is gone, but that booze is a sneaky little shit— the disease is known to play possum. I've drunk without thinking, so if you can, give it a wide berth. If Tina is there, just be cool—"

"I'm done with that."

"I hear you, but if she *is there*, be cool. Try not to get into any heated, or even heavy, conversations. If you can be helpful, great. The trick is— especially when you're new, don't get agitated. We don't want you doing anything that'll bring the thought that a drink will fix this out of the closet. We'll work on getting you comfortable with being uncomfortable later— that's advanced twelve-step stuff."

"Any other orders, *Carnal*?"

"These aren't orders, they're suggestions. But while I'm at it, why don't you call me later and go to the meeting tonight?"

"Will you be there?"

"I should be, but if I'm not, it shouldn't matter to you."

"Okay."

"And Albert?"

"Yes, *Jefe*?"

"Don't be a dick."

WITCH

Jacob and C.C. were sitting at the family table— a cup of heavily sugared and creamed coffee for Jacob, and a stack of banana pancakes for C.C. Perplexed, Krystal stood at the sink— a half-eaten protein bar clutched in her hand.

"What the hell is all over this counter? Ceace, were you getting into the salt?" She took a sponge across the cutting board. "It's all over the fucking place."

James whispered to C.C. "—at least she's not burning."

"What did you say— did you do this?"

"Yeah, sorry Krys," He kicked C.C.'s foot. "—I thought that lid felt a little loose. Want me to clean it up?"

"No, I got it. You're gonna be late."

He got up and gave C.C. a kiss, grabbed his keys, and turned toward the door. "—I'll see you guys later."

C.C. took ahold of his jacket. "—What about Mommy? She needs a kiss."

"Daddy's in a hurry, Ceace."

"Kisses make things better. Do it!"

Krystal offered Jacob her cheek. He kissed her and then ruffled C.C.'s hair. "—Happy now?"

C.C. took a big bite of pancake, the syrup cascading down her chin.

As Jacob left the house, Krystal returned to her clean-up. "—What the hell, Ceace? He got salt all over the sideboard."

Jacob was gone.

*****

On Thursdays, a few of the women from the hall visited Bayside. The female clients weren't required to interact with the outsiders, but the caseworkers suggested it with extreme prejudice. Connie had abstained until today, and now she found herself on a bench in the garden with a woman who had eight years of sobriety— Beverly, the owner of a small flower shop on the beach road. They sat knee-to-knee.

"Why couldn't I see it before?"

"Don't be so hard on yourself, Connie. We can see when we can see."

"I know, but it's not just my kids not wanting to see me, it's everything— my drinking, my husband. I just don't understand how I could be so blind. I'm so embarrassed. How did they put up with me?"

"I asked myself that same question— which I consider a good thing. Self-entitlement, coupled with alcoholism, is about as ugly as it gets. It's good to be repulsed by our past behaviors— especially when they're so horrendous. Let it hurt."

Connie didn't bother hiding the tears. It was too late for that. She sobbed unhindered until Beverly spoke.

"I remember when I woke up. It was Christmas. I was decorating our tree. My grandmother had passed down a beautiful Victorian ornament— enamel with gold filigree, and I kept it in a special box. I set my glass of wine down— ready to hang that trinket, but when I opened the box, it was empty. I looked at my husband. I was about to berate him for being so careless with that treasure, and when my eyes met his, I remembered. I broke that ornament. I was drinking. I stumbled into the tree and I smashed it. I still have the scars on my palm from where the glass was removed— thirteen stitches. Do you know I'd wrecked two cars and had three drunk drivings before I'd opened that box? My children weren't speaking to me, and I was on the verge of another divorce. I'd smashed my whole life, and yet, it took that missing ornament to make me see it."

"Do they speak with you now?"

"David does. Charlotte still won't take my calls."

"I don't know what to do."

"You already did the hardest part— you woke up."

"But what if they never speak to me again?"

"You hold true to a course, regardless. No matter what they do, or don't do, you work your program. These things take time, Connie. One of the biggest lies in recovery is when people say that our families will return. That's just not true. Some of them don't. Some through death never will. Don't stay sober for them, that's conditional sobriety. But know this— sober you have a chance. Drunk, you don't."

There was an hour before lunch— free time to be spent at the client's discretion. *Her book* was waiting on the nightstand. Emily was away at the doctor's— *finally, a few moments of solitude... alone, with my thoughts... ughhh, probably not the best company. I need to get out of this crap. What the hell did they say, service, service, service?*

She cut through the break room. The tables were not yet bussed from morning snack. She emptied the refuse into the trash can, scraped the plates, and stacked them by the sink. She wiped the tables, and as she was stacking the chairs, Richard the Duke of Double-Scrub pushed a mop bucket into the room. He tilted the wooden handle in her direction.

"If you make sure it's as dry as possible— squeeze out the excess, it won't make such a mess."

She ran the mop-head through the strainer and took a swipe. Richard walked out to his cart and returned with a spray can and a squeegee. He did the windows as Connie mopped the floor.

LUNCH DATE

"You know, if somebody wanted to poison you, they'd know just where to put it. Every time, the same fucking thing."

They sat at Alan's usual table— number eight. James swore that if the old man died, they'd hang his picture on the wall above the booth. Alan was enjoying his usual— dry meatloaf, cranberry-side, coleslaw, and home fries.

"First off, I've outlived everyone that ever hated me— except maybe that Tuesday night secretary. He's a real asshole. Second, I like eating the same thing— I've been snacking on my wife for over fifty years and she's still delicious." He put down his fork and took a drink of soda— cherry cola with three cherries and two straws. "So, you knew I was a traveling salesman, right?"

"No," James rolled his eyes. "You've never told me that."

"Okay, smartass— and speaking of being poisoned, that grilled-cheese-on-raisin has been laying across your plate since I first met you, and not only is it your regular, it's just not right."

"Oh, somebody is off their Geritol this afternoon. Is it time for a nap?"

"If I may, I'm trying to enlighten you. Years back, traveling salesmen— there was this stretch of highway— it might've been the 10, or the 40, or the 66. Shit, I can't remember, but every hundred miles or so, you'd see this sign saying, 'See the Bear.' In those days you could treat an animal like that— confine a wild bear to a cage. Now, this cage measured six feet deep and eight across, and that's how that bear moved— day after day. He'd walk a couple feet up, turn, walk twice that again, and then turn, six feet up, eight across— up and back.

The people running that roadside stand fed him, and they cared for him in their own way, but he lived in that enclosure. He was an oddity and a prisoner. Day after day, families on their travels would stop to see the beast. They laughed at him and poked him with sticks. The kids would often torment him— throwing trash and mimicking his rage. When the bear was younger, he'd growl and roar at the agents of his abuse. But soon, he accepted their harassing taunts with a depressed resignation. And day after day, he'd walk six feet up and eight back— six and eight. One day, a group came and rescued the bear. They took him to a beautiful sanctuary in the hills. There were streams and tall pines, clean air, good food, and above all, finally, a chance of peace. When they opened the cage, the bear stepped from his confines. A cool breeze swept over him. There were miles on either side that he could travel— a universe to explore. But then... that great bear slowly lowered his head. He exhaled a deep breath of new air, and then he walked six feet up, and eight back— six and eight."

"Where are you going with this, man?"

"Nowhere, just talking."

"Bullshit. You never say anything without a reason. What are you doing?"

Alan finished his soda. He held up his glass for a refill. "I was thinking about your mother. I was wondering if you were going to pursue that resentment any further."

"I pursued it to the point that I accept she's sick."

"And what does that do for you?"

The waitress brought Alan another— "Thanks sweetheart."

James waited until the server walked away, his sandwich getting cold on the table. "I let it go."

Alan took a sip. He speared a cherry with his straw— "Okay. How's your sandwich?"

James stared at his plate. "What do you want me to fucking do, man? She'll be dead soon. I'll be free." He pushed his meal away. "You fuckers told me to look at her like she's sick, well, she's fucking sick, okay? I get it."

Alan speared another cherry, swirled it around the bottom of his glass. "Sometimes we think we've let stuff go, but we're only fooling ourselves— going through the motions."

He offered the cherry to James. He didn't accept it.

"How's that boy doing— the James Dean-looking kid with that red jacket— another rebel without a clue, huh?"

"He's doing okay."

"Do you got a word count on that? I see you talking and talking and talking— are you getting anywhere?"

"Yeah, I guess. You know how it goes."

"I do. You know, you not believing in God has never bothered me. I say the Rosary for you anyway— every night. I watch you question the existence of the Lord, but then, I don't know if I've ever seen someone try to adhere to the New Testament as closely as you do. You quote scripture more than my fucking priest— excuse my mouth. But the other day, I got to thinking. If you don't have a God to rely on, who does the heavy lifting? You're not trying to save that boy on your own, are you?"

"Come on, man. I'm not new. I know I don't have the power to save that kid. I'm just giving him what I've got. You know me better than that."

"Did I ever give you my take on the fourth step— the flaws in it?"

"No."

"The trouble with 'a fearless moral inventory,' is, the confessing alcoholic only writes what he sees— he outlines the resentments, the defects, and the wrongs. If he doesn't see it, he doesn't list it, and it goes undiscovered."

"You're getting senile, old man. That's my theory. I told you that."

"Yes, you did."

LET'S GET IT ON

He tried pushing the volume, but it couldn't go any higher. The speakers were pumping fuzz-fueled punk rock to the limit of their existence. He was killing it. His truck was back on the road— running better than before, things were moving along at home, and this had to be the best song he'd ever heard.

They got weak on that last record— dipping into that synthesizer crap, but fucking-a, this is the shit!

He was pounding on the steering wheel and running dark yellow traffic lights. No booze, no blow, no weed— this was life on the natural and it couldn't be better. He skidded into the driveway, clipped C.C.'s bike with his tire, and when he shut down the stereo, he could still hear it thumping in his head.

He walked tall toward the house.

I'm starting to feel like a fucking man again. Yeah, I'm still on the couch, but it won't be long now. My rizz is wicked strong— borderline gaslighting, but who wouldn't try to wiggle their way into forgiveness? Besides, I mean it, I'm a new man!

He was whistling as he opened the front door and stepped into a disco love-in. Krystal was sitting on the floor. She was wearing a long hippie sundress, and surrounded by her albums. There was a smoky incense haze in the room and it felt like something magical might happen.

He said hello, but she stood up without replying— *fuck, she's got that fucking Bette Midler out— baby making music.*

Krystal dropped the needle on track one, 'Do You Want to Dance?'— a smooth disco rendition of the old Bobby Freeman tune. She held out her arms.

"Shit, come on, Krys."

"Shut up."

She pulled him close as the song began. His arms, without thought, wrapped around her. She put her head on his shoulder. Her perfume, like heaven, sang, *"Do you want to dance and hold my hand? Tell me you're my lover, man."*

"—I'm sorry, Krys. I really am."

"Not now, Jacob."

They slow-danced in the living room, the tension in their embrace lifting with the groove, the resentment of months dropping with the beat. He buried himself against her.

I knew it, man. Stay tight, and it'll be all right. That's my song, baby.

The door to C.C.'s room opened just enough for a small girl to spy, and for the renewal of their love to entice her. Her parents were lost in each other as she opened the door wider— the incense and song swirling in. Wider, enough for her to step into the living room.

As the song climbed into a crescendo, she burst upon their world. C.C. ran from the doorway and wrapped her arms around her parent's legs— her sweet voice joined in song, the three of them dancing— a family again. Jacob lifted her into his arms. He danced with his daughter as Krystal hovered near, eyes closed, still grooving— *"Hug me, kiss me baby, all through the night."*

That evening they slept in the big bed— from the left, Jacob, Skrunchy, Kiggles, Burt, C.C., and Krys.

He woke with a smile on his face. Still fully dressed— he hadn't expected to be allowed to stay, his shoes were on the floor beside him, and the song still playing in his head. He walked into the bathroom— quiet, as not to disturb C.C. and Krystal. Taking off his clothes, he turned on the shower, and brushed his teeth— *"do you, do you…"* He couldn't get it out of his head so he surrendered— *"do you want to dance with me baby."* He was dancing as Krys opened the door. She stepped inside and locked it behind her. She pulled the dress over her head, and stepped out of her panties. The toothbrush fell to the floor as he pushed her against the wall— kissing her with a mouthful of morning spring mint. She pushed back, wrapping her body around his.

THERAPY

Therapists often need therapy more than their clients do. She could talk to James, and she had friends and a sponsor, but some burdens were better dumped on a stranger.

"I heard her voice— there was a long time that I could only remember her face, but last week, as I was standing on the balcony, listening to the waves, avoiding an extremely manic James, I heard her speak."

"Can you recall her words?"

"'Loser, bitch, junkie.' She called me a slut for cheating on her father. She never forgave me for that."

She saw Dr. Marks once a month, sat on his couch, tore through his Kleenex, and cleansed her soul. The conversations were usually about her relationship, and her father, but recently they included her daughter.

"Is there an argument against those words— the things she said to you?"

"No. I was exactly as she said. I wanted to be a good mother. I tried— that's a lie. I apologize. She was a burden. I was angry when I found out I was pregnant, but Gary wanted children, so I went along with it. I stayed clean for most of the pregnancy, but I was high a couple of days after she was born. I was in and out of sobriety until she died."

"Do you feel imprisoned by her death, the loss of her?"

"As sick as it sounds, I felt relief. She had become me— the abusive boyfriends, the missing for weeks at a time, the begging for help and then turning her back on her rescuers. She'd overdosed twice and the third time was the end. I was in a meeting when I heard the news. My ex came to the club and tore me apart in front of my friends— although, he didn't say anything that they didn't already know. I lived off their sympathy. I fed from their attention and kindness. I used their love to get by and after a year or so it hit me. I lost my little girl. And now I *do* feel imprisoned by it. I can't repair it. I can't save her. I live in it sometimes, believing that I'm still what she said— even though my life today runs contrary to my daughter's words. I constantly wish I could go back as I am now and be that mother for her."

"How long ago did you lose her?"

"Margaux died on my sixty-third day of sobriety. That was almost ten years ago. She was only seventeen."

"I can't imagine the pain you've had to endure— the death of your father, the loss of your daughter. Has losing them affected you in other areas— in your present relationship?"

"It's hard to go to work some days. I want to stay next to James, breathe him in, and not let go. I don't want to lose him and I strangle him with my fear. I'm jealous, accusing. I think someone is going to take him away from me, so I act out."

"Does James ever contradict those thoughts, or do his actions confirm them?"

"He says I'm crazy. He's never done anything to harm me. He's always kind— for all his faults, he's a good man, and I believe he loves me."

Talking about Margaux was hard. I only knew of my father as an alcoholic. I'd never seen him sober. He was always in poor health. His death expected, if not late in coming. Margaux was my baby— innocent and pure. The rise of her addiction caught me unaware, and she was gone before I realized just how bad it had become. I know grief takes time, but James often says, if you feel bad enough long enough, you're going to stick something in you to make it go away. I don't want that.

She was driving back to work when James called.

"Hey sweetheart. What's up?"

"My mom had a stroke— it's pretty bad, I guess."

"When did it happen?"

"Day before yesterday. Nobody bothered to call. My sister went to check on her— found her on the floor."

"Is she going to be alright?"

"I'm not sure. You can't get a straight story out of these fuckers, but she's still breathing."

"Okay, you're there now? I'll drive over— let me cancel my ten o'clock and I'll see you in a bit. You at Memorial or County?"

"I'm at County, but don't worry about it. I'm okay. I'm gonna hang out for a while— try to get a look at her, and then I'm taking off. I'm supposed to swing by the hall and do the floors."

"Sweetheart, get someone else to do it. You do enough over there."

"And that's why I'm still sober. I can't do anything here. I'd rather put my head into service."

"You know that's bullshit, James. You can't hide your feelings in a meeting."

"Yeah, I can."

He was dragging his heels— hanging out in the hallway of the hospital, head-nodding at strangers, and watching a work crew tear up a street across the parking lot. He took out his phone and called Jacob.

"Hey, buddy, what's happening? You wanna help me do the floors today?"

"At the hall?"

"Yeah— once every six months, whether they need them or not."

"I'd be down, but I signed up for overtime. I'm trying to catch up— get the man off my back, yeah?"

"I hear you. I'm glad things are going good down there, but don't forget how you got there. You gotta stay clean to keep it."

"I know. I'm juggling, but I know what keeps the balls in the air. Hey, don't steal that line. That's some good thinking, huh? I'm gonna use it at the hall."

"Yeah, you do that."

He still wasn't ready to go in so he took an elevator to the lobby.

I should get her some flowers, but she says they're a waste of money— ha! Fuck it. I'll get 'em anyway, peonies, she hates those. A little bouquet of 'fuck you' while she's down.

He sent an arrangement anonymously.

On the way back up, he called Albert.

"Beto! Hey, I've gotta do the floors today. You wanna give me a hand?"

"Of course, man. When do you need me?"

"Three o'clock... you know, you could've fought me on it. A bit of resistance isn't bad."

"I've ceased fighting, James."

"Ughhh, you gotta slow up on that book, dude. Do me a favor, give me one 'fuck you' just so I know you're not going soft on me!"

"No way, man."

"Sponsor's direction."

"You're not my sponsor, you made that very clear. We're only friends— shoulder to shoulder. But James?"

"Yeah?"

"Fuck you." Albert hung up.

James' mother was breathing with the help of a tube.

I've never seen her so peaceful, so childlike. I don't know what you've been doing, darling, but it works.

He laughed, remembering that line from a movie— self-soothing his distress. He pushed back her hair and kissed her forehead. She didn't look her age. The women in his family had legs. They lived well into their nineties as the men died young. James was as old as they came— his father died of alcoholism at fifty-two, his grandfather before that. He stood at the foot of her bed. One remembrance of kindness was what he was trying to find, but the memories of her actions forbade it.

A nurse quietly entered the room and stood beside him.

James wasn't much for silence. "—I never liked her."

"Are you her boy?"

"Yeah."

"Jeez, I get that. At one time, I hated my mother, too. She was so mean-spirited. Beat me something awful."

The nurse tucked his mother's blanket in and adjusted the blinds— "I don't know why I'm telling you this. It's not very professional. I apologize."

James reached out and touched her shoulder. "—I'm not gonna tell on you. I appreciate it. I was trying to recall a kindness, and I was hard-pressed to remember even one."

She checked the ventilator and turned off the light in the bathroom— "Oh, I'm sure they're there— maybe not as many as we might like, but often our hate camouflages their love—" She looked at her watch. The morning shift was coming to a close. "I left North Carolina as soon as I could. I was eighteen years old, fresh out of high school. I took a bus to California. I told my brother where I was going— I felt bad about leaving him in the lurch, but I wouldn't take my mother's calls. I wouldn't have nothing to do with her. I guess I could've changed my number, but it felt good to know she was looking for me and I was hurting her." There was a knock on the door— peonies from downstairs. They put them on a small table in the corner.

"You see, somebody must have thought she was pretty special."
James smiled without words.

"Anyway, it wasn't until she passed that her sister got hold of me—
my Auntie Rose. She wanted to bring me some of my mother's things.
It wasn't much, a locket and an envelope full of old photos— Rose looks
like her, kinda made me sick to my stomach when she walked in.
Anyway, she told me that my mother was the sweetest little girl,
wouldn't hurt a fly, until her daddy put his hands on her in a sexual way.
I guess after my grandfather molested her, she changed. She withdrew,
and she hardened." The nurse pulled a small gold locket from beneath
her scrubs— the light gold chain hanging around her neck. "Look
here— " She opened it, and held it out to James. "That's her on the right,
and who do you think that other is?"

"It's you."

"That's right, I keep the little girls side-by-side." She put the locket
away. "Anyway, I had to sit with that a bit— thinking about how her
daddy did her, and I realized that all that hate and sickness couldn't have
come from one man. Yeah, he was the one who put his hands on her,
but who put their hands on him? He got it from someone else, and they
got it from someone else, and so on, and so on, all the way down that
line. I bet if your mother was rough, it didn't begin with her." She
adjusted the pillow beneath his mother's head. "Do you have children?"

"Yeah, I have a daughter, Annie."

"Does she hate you?"

"No. My little girl loves me."

"That's good to hear… but now I wonder why that hate-line broke
at you? The way things usually go is, unless there's been a shift, sickness
begets sickness."

"I got sober. I've never raised a hand toward my little girl."

The nurse laughed. "You and I are part of the same club, James. I've
been sober a little over fifteen years."

"Fuck—" He hugged her. "I should have known it when you started oversharing."

"And I should've known you were one of us when you said you hated your mother."

They held each other— brother and sister in a family of millions strong.

"You know, James, I got to thinking one day as I was looking at my mother's pictures. There were a few of me and my brother, our old house by the river, our dog— so God-damn scroungy, but none of my mother other than the little girl that I have around my neck. There were no photos of her as an adult. I think she was trying to tell me something. I think she wanted me to remember her before her father had fouled her. She wanted me to see her as a little girl— as a friend."

"Is my mom gonna be alright?"

"I don't know. This isn't my floor. I tried to get up the stairway, but there was a lock on the outer door. I cut down here, saw the door to your mother's room ajar, and I peeped in. You know how God works."

"Yeah, I guess I do."

FREEDOM

Connie was in the breakroom reading as Regina walked in.

"Hey, princess. How's it going?"

The name no longer bothered her. It was a reminder of who she was, who she could still be. "Chopping wood, carrying water."

"What are you reading?"

She wasn't sure. She checked the front cover. "—'Strong Sponsor, Weak God,' by the Reverend Eli Charles, 1943. I found it on the shelf."

"Are you getting anything out of it?"

"The Reverend says I need to cultivate the inner voice— the God within. I'm to work off hunch and inspiration."

"That's pretty heady stuff. Often, our true voice lies beneath our defects of character. Stay sober, clear the way, and that God-voice within will rise. I guess you heard Emily left."

"I don't understand it. She was here for free— she seemed so grateful."

"She was, and then that other voice— the illness talking, told her it was time to go. Her boyfriend picked her up this morning."

Connie took a sip of lemon drink— zero fruit juice. "Hey, Regina, can I ask you something?"

"What's on your mind?"

"Is it hard?"

"What do you mean?"

"I mean, you can see us. You know we're not awake, and you know most of us won't stay sober. If I were you, I'd want to slap the shit out of some of us— especially me."

"If I hadn't learned how to detach, I couldn't do this job. And even so, some days I go home and cry— call in sick, shut down. My partner does her best to comfort me, but it's not enough. The amount of trauma that a person deals with in this business is unbearable. The recovery field is rife with burn-out. You know what her boyfriend did to her, don't you?"

"I saw the scars."

"There's nothing we can do about that. People often use the 'disease concept' with alcoholism, but make no mistake— this is a mental illness. The vast majority of our clients are delusional, and the chances of them waking up are slim to none."

She slid a chair next to Connie. "—You guys are clear until this afternoon, right?"

"We've got the meeting at 6:30, but I'm open until then if you'd like me to do something for you."

"I was thinking of driving down to the hall. They're doing the floors today and I wanted to bring down some donuts or something." She took a sip of Connie's drink, was going to spit it back in the glass, then swallowed it like medicine. "—I was going to go alone, and then my inner-voice said, Connie is doing a great job, ask her to come along."

"Is that how it works?"

"Usually, and I listen if the voice is one of kindness. If it's unselfish, and loving, I follow it— although, I have made mistakes." Regina got to her feet.

"You wanna tell me about that?"

"Another time, princess. I'll go grab you a pass."

"Thanks, Regina. I appreciate what you do here— helping us stay sober."

"And I appreciate that, but you should also thank yourself. You're putting in the work, taking the steps to get better."

"But without God..."

"Connie, God gives thousands of people a push, but most of them coast until they fall over. You started pedaling, girl. Thank yourself for that."

Regina turned to the door.

"Hey, Regina?"

She turned back— "Yeah?"

"I'm sorry for being such a shit."

She looked her client over— maybe the one out of a ten who might make it. "Thanks, Connie. It's people like you that keep me moving."

A TRIM

As Albert drove down the main boulevard there was a ghost on every corner— an arrest here, a robbery there, the empty field near Jackson High where he ditched his first stolen car, the gas station on 117th where he beat down Lil Rustler, the taco stand on Chavez where he caught his first kiss and his first feel and his first broken tooth compliments of Cindy Marquez's older brother— *yeah, it fucking hurt, but that pussy was worth it. I'd take a pop in the mouth any day for that shit. Besides, I paid him back later, and this gold cap puts enamel to shame.* He smiled in the rearview— *gangster, gangster.* His grandmother would be sad they'd tore down the old *carnicería,* but the liquor store where he bought his first bottle was doing quite well.

I've been reading that blue book, checking out those steps— making the list of my wrongs isn't gonna be a problem— some of them are hard to forget, but facing those fools is gonna be crazy. Gonna have to talk to James about that. I don't want to get shot for being sober.

He was daydreaming when the car in front of him stopped short. He slammed the brakes. A familiar looking man had stepped carelessly into the street and then disappeared into the barber shop on the corner.

I think that was that fucking, Angel. I know it was.

Albert swung around. He parked and called James. No answer. He called again. No answer— *motherfucker. He was all over that phone earlier and now he can't pick it up.* He called again— nothing.

The plastic Jesus on the dash caught his attention. "I guess I'm calling you now. Do I go in, or do I leave?" He closed his eyes. No answer. He listened harder. "—Come on, man. I'm right here. I need you." Jesus said nothing.

He tried James again— straight to voicemail.

Fuck it. Let it go, Beto. Just let it go— you'll get him next time.

The truck next to him inched forward and then jammed on its brakes. A loud bang forced Albert to look in its direction. The slogan 'Just Do It' was printed on the side of the trailer in two-foot letters.

He shut off the Monte and stepped out. "—Okay, loud and clear, Jesus. Just do it. I'm going in."

The barber was cutting Angel's hair as Albert opened the door— a bell announced his presence.

"Hey, Beto— you're not on the book."

Angel looked up in fear. A bandaged cut on his forehead, a healing jagged slash across his cheek.

Albert ignored the barber. He focused on the task at hand. "Hey, Angel. I want a word with you, man."

In the corner, a children's cereal commercial was playing on the TV— the sound too loud for background static. It stole Albert's attention. The young boy reminded him of himself.

The old barber put him back on track. "I don't need any trouble in here, Beto. He's in the chair. This is neutral ground for you guys. You know that."

Albert shot the old barber a 'get real' look. His reputation as a violent, sadistic animal had slipped his mind— fear had always preceded him.

"Angel, I need you to step outside."

"Let me be, Beto."

"If you don't have the balls to come out, I'll do it right here."

The barber ducked behind the counter— his shears falling orphaned to the tiles. Albert stood tall.

"Angel, I want to say I'm sorry for the way I treated you. I'm a fucking asshole sometimes, but I hope you can forgive me. I was angry, and I didn't know how to handle it uh… in a correct way. If there's a way to make it right, I will."

Albert stood unsure of himself. He'd never made amends. He waited for something to happen— nothing. "Okay, then... thank you."

He dusted off his shirt, smoothed the creases— *that wasn't so bad.* He checked the old barber. "—And you should know better, Johnny. I was here for good business."

Angel rose from the chair— the white barber's cape hung from his shoulders.

"I'm sorry too, Albert. I was out of line. The fucking booze talks, and it doesn't shut up, ey?"

"I hear you, man... yap, yap, yap. You know, if you ever need help with that booze talking thing, I'm around."

Albert moved forward and held out his arms. Angel stepped within his grasp and the two adversaries hugged. It was a very masculine affair.

The barber wiped off his shears and patted Albert's back. "—Damn, Beto, that was the best thing I've ever seen. Do you want a free trim?

Albert ran his hand along the side of his neck. The bluebird flashed beneath his fingers. "No, I'm good."

*****

James parked beneath the oak tree near the front lot. There was a lit cigar in his mouth and a slight tremor in his hands. The windows were down and he could hear the voices of the cleaning crew mixing it up in the hall. There was a line he often thought of— an alcoholic is someone who feels homesick for a place he's never been. He felt like that now. He called his daughter.

"Hey, sweetheart."

"Dad?"

"Yeah, who else?"

"You sound strange. You alright?"

"I just called to tell you how much I love you. I think you're wonderful."

"Oh my God, dad. Do you think you're dying again? You're a fucking hypochondriac."

"Thanks, sweetheart. I knew I could count on you."

He watched as Regina shook the dust off a small runner— the piece that was usually by the side table in the back. She should've hit it with the vacuum.

"Dad?"

"Sorry, sweetheart. I just wanted to hear your voice. I love you— and watch the f-bombs, okay?"

"Is that a joke? The guy who told my third-grade teacher to fuck off is telling me to watch my mouth. I'll get right on that."

"Hey, you know she was out of line— fucking control issues, man."

"I gotta go, Dad."

"Okay. I love you."

"You too, Pops. Don't die, don't change, and tell Sarah I said 'hey.'"

She hung up before he could get the last word.

Albert rolled in a few moments after James dropped the call. He was feeling high from his amends. The two men stood in the parking lot: Albert, a new veteran of spiritual wars, and James, an old campaigner ready to school the new man with his past victories.

"I gotta ask you a question, man."

"What's up? You high on the coffee, bro?"

"Come on, dude. You know I've been reading that recovery book, the big blue one."

"And...?"

"The other night that fucking dude said, 'The steps are written in order, made to be done in order...'"

"Yeah, his opinion— not based in fact."

"Well, you said I did steps one, two, and three, but today I jumped to nine. Is that gonna fuck me up?"

"What happened?"

"I saw that fucking Angel on the street, so I made amends to him."

"How'd it go?"

Albert stood proud. "They offered me a fucking haircut."

"What?"

"Did I do it wrong?"

"No, man. You can't do it wrong. What happened?"

Albert laid down the tale like a child returning from school with an 'A' paper.

"That's fucking bitchin, Beto. I wish I was there."

"I said a prayer when I saw him— you didn't answer your phone, so I went to God."

"I'm proud of you— you check your pages. You'll find the part where we roll on a hunch or an inspiration. I'm glad I couldn't answer. I would've done you a disservice if I had. Beto, these days most of these pricks practice fear-based sobriety. They say shit like, 'If you do this you're gonna get drunk, if you do that you're gonna get drunk.' They got these new people so fucked up that they're scared to do anything without going to their sponsor— they can't wipe their asses without a god-damn committee meeting. It's fucking ridiculous. You're gonna make mistakes. You're gonna think you're guided by God and you land in a ditch or pull a fuck-up of epic proportions, but that's okay. We have steps to correct these things. Fucking up doesn't mean drunk. Drunk means drunk, and that's it."

"I hear you, man... but *he* said it with authority."

"There is no authority but the spirit. Being human, and alcoholic, most of us like to control things— oh, we tell people to trust in God, but then we set down rules, and we forget God works between the lines. You can't control the Spirit— mercurial, that's what God is.

"You did steps one through three that night in the parking lot, and you jumped in. You've been checking your behavior— I know you've been praying, and when I asked you to help me, you agreed in a flash. So right there, you're working steps ten, eleven, and twelve. We need to do an inventory and look at those defects, but you're doing this thing. As for amends, it's good to seek wise counsel, so we don't do more damage, but if God rolls the dice, and they land in front of you, you take a deep breath and you dive in. I'm proud of you, man."

"I feel good, James— and I hope you don't get this wrong, but it feels like I just took a drink."

"I hear you— *spiritus contra spiritum,* fucking Carl Jung, man. The spiritual experience— the way your heart feels now, counters the spirits— an old name for booze. Alcohol is a poor imitation of the power of God, and now you're tapping the main thing. Beto, how did you feel when you were a young man and you took that first drink?"

"I felt good."

"And…?"

"Strong, and connected— at one with something."

"Exactly, but it didn't last, did it? It lied to you and look where you ended up."

"Not good."

"No, not at all. Now let me ask you this. How did you feel when you made that amends— Angel, the barber, the trim?"

"I felt good."

"And…?"

"Connected— I felt part of something bigger."

"That's it buddy— that's what we were always looking for, and when you do it this way that feeling doesn't die. The action you took today will blossom and its branches will stretch into places that you never thought of.

"Come on man, let's go get another jolt. Nothing gives greater satisfaction than service gladly rendered. Put a broom in that hand. Let's top this off."

MOVING UP

It was one of those days. Cars were stacked out the door, but appointment or not, Jacob worked them in. His crew was tight, and when necessary, he rolled up his sleeves and lent a hand. At five o'clock, he heard his name called over the intercom. Mr. Grant wanted to see him.

The last time I was in Mr. Grant's office, I was plastered.

He checked the walls. He couldn't remember if he'd punched one or not, but there didn't seem to be any recent damage.

Fucker is living large up here.

The chairs and sofa were top-grain red leather— the polished mahogany desk longer than Jacob's truck. Mr. Grant had windows that looked over the dealership. He could oversee the sales tower and the service bays. Framed dealer awards decorated the walls and a fully stocked bar filled out the room.

"Jacob, I'd move you to sales if I could afford to lose you in the back. Your numbers have surpassed anything we've done in the last four years. I don't know what got into you, but I wish our sales department had a taste of what you're drinking."

An older gentleman walked into the room. Jacob had seen that face a thousand times on billboards and flyers, he had a smile that said, you need a new car and I'm selling. Tom Ivers, owner of Ivers automotive.

"Mr. Jacob," Ivers put out his hand, enfolded Jacob's in a warm embrace. "—I wanted to thank you for your hard work." He pulled out an envelope accompanied by the breath of a seven-martini lunch and handed it to Jacob.

"Thank you, sir."

"Don't give me that 'thank you' shit. Some of you punks drop off when you catch a bonus. Don't do it, son. Tax me, make me come in next month and pay you off again. Grant, I'll see you tonight. Keep it up, kid."

Ivers washed out as fast as he arrived.

Jacob put the envelope in his pocket. "I sure hope he's not driving."

Mr. Grant looked out the window. A blacked-out sedan was idling in the parking lot. "—Looks like he is."

Jacob watched as Mr. Ivers put two orange cones and a sales banner out of their misery.

"He left something for your crew, too." Mr. Grant handed him a small stack of envelopes. "—Make no mistake, Jacob. You're worth the bonus. Keep the old man happy and he'll take care of you."

Jacob whistled the crew together. They were dirty, tired, and ready to go home, but when the envelopes hit their hands, they were reborn.

"You guys are killing it. I don't know what he stuck in those envelopes, but he was hammered, so it should be good."

Charlie, the bay two technician, was the first to open his packet. A crisp hundred-dollar bill and a dinner voucher for Georgia May's Steakhouse and Saloon— "Fucking-a, man!"

The rest of the crew mimicked his sentiment— high fives and straight smiles all around.

"We've got a great crew, guys. The old man said if the numbers stay steady, the cash keeps flowing. Let's take him for all he's got."

A round of applause and the group dispersed... except for Charlie.

"Hey, Jacob. You wanna get a beer with us?"

"Yeah, but I'm not drinking."

"Ha! That's what you said last time!"

"I know, but I fucked up— over served. I'm on the bench for a bit."

"I hear that— you don't mind if I throw a couple back for you?"

"I wish you would. I appreciate the invite. You guys are above and beyond, man."

"Thanks, boss, and hey, if you want a lil' something for later," He tossed Jacob a small poly plastic bag of white powder. "—this'll brighten your day."

As Charlie walked away, Jacob, without thought, tucked the mini-bag in his jacket pocket.

Where were you when I was getting high?

On the way home, he made a decision to flush the blow.

*****

"Hey, mom, can we get an ice cream?" There was a stand outside the restaurant. Sarah, Krystal, and C.C. were having a girls' day out.

"Seriously? We just ate lunch, sweetheart."

"Single scoop— I have my own money."

"Do it." Krystal smiled at Sarah as C.C. ran for the counter. They sat down on a bench. "—where does the money come from? She's eight."

"She's probably shaking down Jacob. How is he?"

"He's been working really hard. I tell him to take it easy, but he knows we're behind from that last bender of his."

"Are you guys getting to any meetings?"

"I am. I've been hitting that Family Afterward group at the hall, but when Jacob gets home, he's too tired. I've tried to get him to go, but he says he has to rest up. I think he's caught a couple, though."

Sarah opened a small compact and touched up her lipstick. "'—God has either removed his liquor problem or he has not...'"

"What did you say?"

"I was thinking of a reading, something James is always going on about. You can't make someone go to meetings, or work a program— you can't shield them, or guide their affairs. Believe me, I tried with my dad. I thought if I just said the right thing, that he'd realize he needed help. But I couldn't come up with that combination of words. I couldn't love him enough, either. He never got it."

"Jacob's a fantastic father. He's doing great. I think this time's different. I can see the change."

C.C. came back with a double-scoop twice the size of her hand. It looked as if she was wearing chocolate lipstick and a strawberry-colored beard.

"There's no way you're taking that in the car. Take a couple of bites and toss it— Sarah has to go."

"I'm okay. I'm gonna make a quick call to James."

C.C. was swallowing fast and hard— an eight-year-old, ice-cream, gutter drunk pounding a pint of Neapolitan ice milk.

"You're gonna freeze your brain, C.C."

Her answer was unintelligible.

I love watching her play— not a care in the world. She has a father that loves her, and I have a great man. Kids are so resilient. We could learn something from them. The bad days seem to slide right off. I wish I could let go so easily.

C.C. was halfway through and still gobbling when Sarah returned.

"He's not answering. Do you mind if we swing by the hall on the way back?"

"Not at all. I'm glad we could get together."

C.C. had tossed the ice cream but the residue coated the door handle and the seat, her shirt, and her pants. She licked the back of her hand.

"I'm glad she's a happy mess. When I was a little girl I was terrified of screwing up— getting spanked for being young. I never wanted to bring friends home."

"Speaking of friends, have you made any at the hall?"

"A couple— they make me feel better about myself, that's for sure."

"What do you mean?"

"A few of them got it real bad. Jacob's never hit me. We pay our bills, and Ceace wears clean clothes to school. There are some real horror stories there."

"Do you think there are different levels of alcoholism?"

"Of course— Jesus, Sarah, some of those women have been to prison."

"I've been to prison."

"I thought it was jail."

"There's a difference?"

"Yeah, I mean Jacob's been to jail."

"Locked up is locked up. I did sixteen months at the state institute for women. I was interned for 'assault with intent to commit great bodily harm,' and drug possession. I was convicted. I'm a convict, and an alcoholic is an alcoholic— whether it's a few glasses of wine in the afternoon or a fifth in an alley. If they want to stop and can't, it doesn't matter how much they're doing, or where they're doing it."

"I'm sorry. I didn't mean anything."

"I know. I just want you to know what and who you're dealing with."

"I know you."

"It's not me I'm talking about. I'm talking about Jacob."

"God— if Jacob ever goes to prison, it's bye-bye! You can count on that."

MOP AND WIPE

James and Albert walked into a heated discussion. A couple of recovered drunks were arguing principles as they mopped the floor.

"Go on, ask James. He'll tell you. You're not supposed to say it."

"Look, Froggy, it says we're not saints. Read the print. I don't gotta ask anybody."

"I know what it says— I'm not new, but you can't say that to yourself. James, tell him."

"What the fuck are you two talking about?"

"Arthur got into it with some dude at the market. The guy backed into Arthur's motorcycle, so Arthur kicked his ass. I told him he was wrong and he said, oh well, we're not saints. Tell him, tell him, he's fucked up."

"Look, you guys do whatever the fuck you want, but I can't justify my shitty behavior by saying, 'oh well, I'm not a saint.'"

"Told you."

"However, so that Arthur doesn't start kicking his own ass for not being perfect, you, as his friend, can comfort him by saying, 'Look Arthur, you're not a saint. We make mistakes, now clean it up.'"

"Told you."

"You guys have to learn to live in the grey— the principles are not fascist. Hey, Cindy—" A twenty-something girl in a pair of coveralls and boots was lugging in chairs. "—what's the prayer we say at the beginning of the meeting?"

"Serenity prayer?"

"That's right, and what are we asking for?"

"Serenity?"

"And…?"

"Wisdom? Courage?"

"Wisdom. Fucking-a right— every fucking day you plead for wisdom— the wisdom to know the difference."

"Yeah, but you don't say it right."

"Oh, Mr. Beto wants to jump into the conversation— enlighten me."

"You say the things that *should* be changed— not can."

"At least you're paying attention. I can change all sorts of things, but should they be changed? When I say 'should,'— which was an earlier version of our prayer, it reminds me about behaviors that I'm currently engaged in that should be altered. Maybe I'm not eating right, getting enough sleep, arguing over trifles; whatever it is, I bring it to the forefront of my mind, and I deal with it. But if I don't stay aware, and invested, that Serenity Prayer is nothing but words."

"Hey, James, do you think this is a disease?"

"Miss Cindy, it doesn't matter what I think."

"But I want your opinion— respect for other people's opinions and viewpoints, you showed me that."

"Hey, I just came over here to do the floors."

"And I'm here for the chairs— come on."

Froggy handed the mop to James and sat down at the piano. James swiped the floor. "—okay, I got no idea if it's a disease. I prefer 'mental illness,' but some people don't like the sound of that. I remember telling my father that I had a disease and he told me that I was nothing but a selfish little fuck who couldn't hold his booze. Some alcoholics use the disease concept as an excuse."

"Are you talking about a social disease?" Froggy banged out a few notes on the old piano and swung into a show tune. "—*Dear kindly Sergeant Krupke, Ya gotta understand: It's just our bringin' upke that gets us outta hand. Our mothers all are junkies, our father's all our drunks— golly Moses, natcherly we're punks!!*"

"There it is!" James and Cindy joined him on the chorus. "—*We are punks, we are drunks, we are sick, sick, drunks, oh we're not crazed you know we're drunks!*"

A round of applause came from the doorway— Krystal, Sarah, and an ice-creamed-faced C.C. had arrived.

"Is that what goes on over here?"

James gave Sarah a kiss and put his hand out to C.C. "—Who's this?"

She offered a sticky hand. "You may call me Ceace, but my real name is C.C. with two C's."

"It's a pleasure to meet you, Miss Ceace. You can fill in for your father while he's at work."

"Can I play the piano?"

"You'll have to fight Froggy for it."

As she ran for the keys, James dipped his hand into the mop bucket and wiped it on his pants— a Pine-sol ice cream remover. "Hey! Wash your hands!"

THE TALK

It was a Saturday night. James was wearing a black suit with a white shirt and no tie. His sleeves were wet, and there was a light coffee-stain on his collar. The pots were rolling— three up and one ready if needed. Albert walked through the back door.

"Fuck, this place is packed, dude. Who's speaking?"

"Some asshole."

"What's with *that*? You don't talk shit, man."

Sarah came in and kissed James on the neck. He shook her off. "You're gonna get lipstick all over my collar. What are you doing?"

"I'm trying to cover the coffee-stain."

She was wearing a tight black dress and her hair was pulled back. She gave Albert a hug. "Hey, Albert. Watch my hand. If I pull my ear like this, it means he's exaggerating."

"Who are you talking about?"

"If James starts blowing up his story, I'll pull my ear."

The Coffee Maker gave her a sweet push. "—Get the fuck out of here. We got work to do."

As Sarah left, James returned to his pots.

"You're speaking, *Carnal*?"

"Just another drunk with a story. We all have 'em, Beto."

"You know, the only one you talk shit on is you. Why is that?"

"'Hard on ourselves, easy on others...'"

"Yeah, I been reading that shit too. That's a fucking cop-out. You do a lot of good work here. You lead like a soldier, not a general— shoulder to shoulder." Albert bumped knuckles with James but then he stopped and held out his arms. "—Come on, *Carnal*."

"You ready for that?"

"Come on." Albert and James embraced in the kitchen. "Do me a favor, okay? Be good to yourself. You helped save my life."

*****

She let C.C. tie the ribbon in her hair— a bright yellow bow. This was the happiest she'd felt in years. She'd told Sarah she'd be a greeter at the meeting and she wanted to look her best. Jacob walked into the room still wearing his work clothes. He kissed her on the cheek.

"Jacob, where's the sitter? We gotta go."

"I'm not going."

"What? Your sponsor is speaking."

Jacob walked Krystal to the side, out of C.C's earshot. His red jacket hung on a chair in the living room.

"I know. I'm on sponsor's orders. I forgot to tell you. James said I should stay home. I owe C.C an amends, and it's time to make it. We're gonna color and bake cookies, and I'm gonna watch whatever she wants. I owe her, baby."

Krystal kissed him. "—Will you be up for me when I get home? You can make amends to me, too."

He pulled her close, his lips against hers, his hands wrapped familiar around her waist, their bodies touching. "You know I will."

"I wish I could stay home with you."

"Go on— do your thing. I'll be waiting— and if I'm asleep, you know how to wake me."

She kissed him again. "You're a good daddy, Jacob."

*****

The room was packed. There was nervous excitement in the air. James was one of their own— he was the coffee maker, and they knew what they were in for.

"Good evening, I'm James and I'm an alcoholic."

The crowd returned the greeting and then a lone voice rose from the back. "—thank yourself for coming out!"

The crowd laughed.

"It never stops does it, Alan? Fifty years sober and you're still yelling out shit from the back?

"You get fifty and then we'll talk— newcomer!"

"Okay then… I'm James, and I am an alcoholic, and I love being sober, and I love being here, and— " the recovered alcoholics in the room joined him on the last line. "—I want to thank myself for coming out."

Applause and laughter shook the humble walls of their home.

It's imperative to have a family— not of origin, but of choice. Go where the love is, they told me, and I am loved here. If I could say anything to a new man— besides grow up, I would stress the importance of community. The church is the people. It's not the walls that enclose us, it's the love that frees us.

"Thank you, Alan." He smiled at the old man and then took the room in with his gaze— *all inclusive.* "And I want to thank you, and I sure hope that when you're thanking God, or whatever power you're claiming, that you thank yourself too, because I guarantee that without your will, your thoughts, and your actions, God won't do a damn thing to help you succeed. Now hold up. I see some of you looking like you just sucked on a lime, and we don't want to start like that. Let me give you a take. When I was a boy, and I was doing schoolwork— which I was never very good at, and if I had to write a report— which I was also not very good at— I'd ask my mother for help, and after some crying and pleading and a spanking or two, she would grudgingly write the first word and then tell me I had to take it from there.

"I remember the way she held the pen against the paper, how her ring would often twist off center and how she touched it when she was nervous. I remember the scent of her white wine breath on my pages.

"My mother would get me going, but she wasn't gonna write it for me. I believe God works in the same way. After some crying and pleading and a spanking or two, God will give you that flash of a new life— that spark of awakening, but He will not write it for you. You've gotta create that on your own, and when you've written a couple of nice lines— a good relationship with your partner, and your children, a comfortable appreciation of life, then I challenge you to look in the mirror and say thank you. Thank you for doing the work."

He smiled at Sarah and for a moment thought about stepping down from the podium and hiding in her arms…

"My mother is on her way out. Oh, I know we're all dying— some of us sooner than others, but as I stood over her hospital bed, I realized that she was done. And then, in true alcoholic fashion, I'm standing there thinking, what am *I* gonna get out of it— *my* legacy."

Laughter filled the room.

"And then it hit me. She'd already given me what I had coming. She gave me a gift that would never shrink, never become depleted, and if anything, it was a gift that would grow throughout the years. It had legs of its own. You see, my mother had passed down the legacy of resentment. I hated her for the physical and emotional abuse that I'd suffered— just as she had hated her mom. That was my gift. That's what she gave me.

"I told Alan the other day that when my mother died, I'd be free. You know what his response was? He said, 'Okay' —that's it, one word. He knew I wasn't going anywhere, and when she died, that cage of resentment— that hate, would still surround me. I needed to let it go. But I couldn't. You know, for people that are so good at shaking up their lives, you'd think we'd be better at casting off things that don't serve us. But oh, no. Our minds lock on to the pain and we embrace it. We will hurt, and re-hurt, and re-hurt, until it fucking kills us. And then we sit in these meetings— crying like a baby, and some fucking clown yells out 'surrender!' As if *he* knew how. Surrender is an instinct non-human. As an animal, I am not built to let go. It goes against my very nature of survival. I can't consciously surrender. I will fight until I am destroyed.

"I often tell people that our program doesn't work, and I know some of you have gotten upset with me for that. But my opinion hasn't changed. Our program does not work *unless* 'something from beyond our control,' power, or plan touches us.

"The other day, as I was looking at my mom in that hospital bed— thumbing through a litany of past hurts, a nurse by mistake walked into the room— my new friend Effie May."

He winked at Effie, sitting in the front row next to Sarah.

"She shared her story with me and through that, I could see my mother as a child, as a little girl who had only wanted to be loved and protected, and the world had conspired against her. My mother wasn't evil. She was hurt. And she was doing the best she could. In an instant— seeing her that way, thinking of her as a child, I forgave her. I wish I could have held her and told her it was gonna be okay.

"You see, it wasn't enough for me to see her as a sick person— as our literature instructs. I had to see her *before* she became ill. Whatever that was, that thing, that force, that propels our program— without which it will not work, Nurse May carried it into that room, and it entered me with her words, and it destroyed my legacy of hate. The invisible cage that I had built around me had disappeared. I was free to love her."

"I remember her favorite dress, the shoes she wore, her lipstick shade, her matching purse, and the scent of spice in her perfume when she walked into a room. I loved my mother and I just wanted her to love me in return.

"You'll often hear in these rooms that you have to do the work, but none of us can tell you what that work is. These steps are not the work; they are a way of life. The work is releasing the sickness that clouds our souls. For some of us, our work is to learn how to share. For others, it could be how to love, how to be disciplined, or like me, how to let go of resentment and to stop hating yourself so fucking much— for some of you, that work might be repairing an old wound. I had to learn that I was worthy of love, even though she was incapable of giving it."

He stood for a moment, checking that he had said all that was required for the message to be conveyed.

"I want to welcome those who are new. I hope you're done, that you know in that innermost self that you will never find peace in your addiction, that peace must come from within. I wanna thank you for having me."

The applause swelled as the meeting ended. Effie May walked to the podium and put her arms around James. Alan came from the back and joined them. Love surrounded him.

$$*****$$

"If you flip the big chair over, we can push it against the table and cover it with a blanket."

He did as she said. She was better than him. Her fort skills were top-notch. The dining room table could withstand any assault.

"You sure we shouldn't have a bite of chicken fingers before your mom gets home?"

"No. You said, 'what I want' and dinner was what I want." There were two plates on the counter— chocolate chip cookies, gummy worms, and Sour Patch grape. He felt sick.

"I need air, sweetheart— time-out."

He put on his jacket and went outside. They had a nice yard— *Krys was talking about some kind of water feature, but who knows where she wants to stick it, or what it's gonna cost me. A pool would be nice— or a hot tub— sudsy bubbles. I could get with that. That was a tight little bonus I pulled down. A couple more of those and Krys could put a fucking pond back here.*

Jacob couldn't see it, but the moon was reflecting off his tiara and when he lit a cigarette, there was a warm glow in his eyes. It was colder than he thought. He held the smoke in his mouth and put his hands in his jacket pockets—*what the fuck is that? Oh... fucking Charlie. I thought I tossed that.*

"Dad, come on!"

He took a few more puffs and then he flicked the still-lit cigarette into a small pile of wet leaves. He watched as the smoke slowly rose and made its way up the side of the house, over the sill, and out of sight.

I didn't think C.C. would ever go down— fort-building, hide and seek, beauty parlor, dancing with Burt the Dragon— God-damn it. She finally passed out and I carried her to bed. I watched her sleep for a moment— kissed her on the cheek, brushed the crumbs from her face, and then I went into the kitchen and cleaned up. It was getting colder. I'm a lucky man.

He put on his jacket and stepped outside. Krys would be home soon.

COMING DOWN

James was lying on top of the covers. He had on his favorite pajamas— red-checked flannel, and a pair of fuzzy pink socks pulled half-way off his feet, the way he liked to wear them. His thoughts were miles and years away.

"Well, that wasn't your standard talk."

He smiled at her— a schoolboy chastised by kindness.

"I love you, James."

She crawled on top of him, spread her legs, and pinned him to the covers. She kissed him gently on the lips. Her phone rang. She reached for it.

"Leave it."

She sent the call to voicemail, but a second later it rang again.

"Come on Sarah, I'm trying to get comforted here."

Again, she put the call to voicemail, was about to hit 'do not disturb' and it rang again. This time she answered. "—Hey, you're on speaker. What's up?"

"Jacob's not here. I came home, and no one was watching C.C."

"Are you guys okay?"

"His fucking truck is gone. He left the baby."

"He probably ran to the store or something—"

"At ten at night?"

James pushed her away and got off the bed.

"Was C.C. up when you came in?"

"No, I woke her."

James put on a pair of pants and pulled his socks up. He mouthed the words 'let's go' as he pulled a t-shirt over his head. Dressed and ready, he was waiting for her.

"Okay, Krys, hold tight. We're coming."

The lights were on. Krystal's car was in the driveway and the front door was open as if they were expecting a visitor. She was waiting in the entryway, her car keys in her hand.

"This is the last fucking time. I swear to God, he's such a fucking asshole."

Sarah steered Krystal toward the kitchen as James checked on C.C. She was sitting with her back against the couch— head down, slightly rocking, talking to Mr. Kiggles.

"Hey, Miss Ceace."

She looked up at him— withdrawn and distant. It was a look he remembered from the mirror of his youth. He forced a smile. It was incomplete and did little to comfort her. He squeezed the doll's hand and went to the kitchen. Sarah was being force-fed the details.

"What happens when you call him?"

"His fucking location is off. It goes straight to voicemail."

James leaned against the counter. "—You know, when my phone dies, it does the same. I'm not saying he's not fucking up, but—"

"Fuck him! I'm fucking over it! Can you change these locks?"

They both knew that arguing was futile. She needed to vent, and they needed to listen without condoning or attacking. After a few moments of Krystal's uncontested angry rambling, Sarah spoke. "Why don't you and C.C go to bed? You can't do anything now."

"Fuck if I can't. I got a good idea where he is, but I need your help."

"Krystal, why don't you—"

"Will you watch C.C. for me?"

"Come on, Krys. Let's take a walk. James can wait here."

"Fuck that. I'm gonna find him and I don't want to drag C.C. down there. Please help me."

Sarah followed her out. James stayed behind.

They cruised the stockyards— an area of seedy motels, streetwalkers, and homeless encampments.

"How could he fucking do this? It's his fucking daughter. Anything could've happened... James called it. He just got a fucking promotion. We were talking about a swimming pool— 'I love you, baby. I love you.' He's so full of shit. I fucking hate him!"

They crossed an underpass and circled down to the river road.

"What makes you think he's here?"

"Because this is where the losers are."

The Liberty, the 777, and the Ali Baba were all fruitless stops. Sarah hoped Krystal would toss it in— they were running out of places to look.

"You know, Krys, there's nothing we can do to make him quit. When my ex—"

"There's his truck. Right there. I fucking told you. I'm gonna beat his fucking ass."

He was parked behind the Sundown Inn. Krystal blocked his truck with her car. She jumped out and kicked a dent in his door. "—Fucking loser. See? Loser."

There was a woman arguing with a cab driver as they approached the after-hours window— another drama unfolding in the parking lot. Krystal pounded on the night buzzer as the cab and the woman drove away.

The night clerk had seen better days— thick coke-bottle glasses, greasy comb-over, dirty t-shirt hiding under a faded college sweater.

"What room are the losers in?"

The clerk said nothing. He tooth-picked his remaining teeth.

"Jacob Stanz, where is he?"

"I can't give out that information."

"I'm his fucking wife!"

"Then you should know where he fucking is."

Sarah had been hanging back— calm, observing, but something in the way he talked to Krystal fingered an old unhealed wound. "Hey, clown. You should watch your fucking mouth."

"I'd rather watch yours, baby."

She stepped up. "Listen, you dickless creep, I'll burn your fucking hotel down." She punched the thick plexiglass window. "—Give me the fucking room number."

The clerk picked up the phone.

"You think I'm fucking with you? Whoever you're calling can't get here fast enough."

"I'm calling the cops, you fucking pyscho."

Sarah was looking for a way into the office when she saw Jacob's name on a registration card. "Krys, he's in 7!"

Krystal ran toward the room as Sarah slowly followed— a few deep breaths and a chance to regain her composure—*calm yourself, bitch.*

Room 7 had been assailed before. The door showed recent heel marks, and the wood was broken and repaired. The air-conditioner was running full blast— a puddle of water forming beneath it. There was a dim light in the room and the torn curtains allowed thin glimpses in.

Krystal tried the locked door. "Jacob! Open the fucking door! Jacob!" She pressed her face against the window and yelled through the glass. "Jacob! I can fucking see you! Open the fucking door!"

He was sitting up on the bed, his head resting against the headboard.

Krystal hammered the door again as Sarah looked through the window. There was no movement. She pounded on the glass and then stepped back. There was a trashcan by the ice machine. She slammed it into the window. The glass shattered. He didn't move. She used the lid of the can to clear the way. Removing the unbroken shards, she climbed in followed by Krystal.

Jacob was still and grey, lifeless, silent. Krystal pounded on his chest as Sarah ran to the office.

"Jacob! Jacob!"

The screams fell behind her as she dialed 911 and yelled at the clerk— "Narcan! Come on, man, give me your kit!"

"Why the fuck would I have that?"

"Fucking tool."

She ran back to the room. Krystal was still holding Jacob, her head against his chest. Sarah pushed her out of the way but it was too late. She administered chest compressions until the paramedics arrived, but Jacob was gone.

I sat on the stairway as the police took Krystal's information. It was matter-of-fact— business as usual. The night clerk was more concerned with the loss of a room, than that of a life— 'that window wasn't broke when they got here. Somebody's gotta pay.' The woman in the cab returned. There was a fight across the street and as the evening progressed, there would be three more overdoses and a fatal stabbing on 22nd. The paramedics took Jacob's body. James would pick up his truck in the morning. I drove Krystal home. There was nothing left to say...

FAMILY

The house was full. Members from the hall had brought food and love. There were children to play with C.C. and the chores were done. Krystal and Sarah sat at the kitchen table.

"I can't breathe."

"I know, sweetheart."

"He was doing so good. I don't understand it— he made her cookies. How could he leave us?"

"He didn't intend to die, Krystal— none of them do."

"But he lied to me— he said James told him to stay."

"Mom?"

"Yeah, Ceace?" She lifted her daughter onto her lap and put her cheek against her head, inhaling the innocence of her.

"Can Mr. Kiggles go with Daddy?"

"Sweetheart, Daddy's gone."

"I know but… can he be with him just in case?"

"Yeah, baby. We'll take him tomorrow." She tightened her hold on C.C.—"Sarah, will you go with us?"

"You don't have to ask. I'll be here in the morning— if you'd like, I could stay."

"Please."

The tears again were uncontrollable, driven by anger and loss.

By early evening, the visitors were gone— James being the last to leave. There were promises of comfort and calls to be made, a community to support her.

She set Sarah up on the couch and then she tucked C.C. in. They were sleeping in the same bed and would be for some time. As she pulled the covers up she could smell him— his scent still on the pillows and the sheets. His soiled work shirt was on the chair, his jacket in the closet, and his shoes placed beside the bed. She would never let them go.

*****

Connie was sitting on the bed when Regina knocked on the door. She'd been allowed her make-up, and it was a different face that greeted the counselor.

"Wow."

"Don't start, Regina. I know it's an inside job, but I feel better when my outside is looking like my inside should." She held out a lipstick tube. "—check this, 'Summer Blush,' to go with my new attitude."

"You're crazy, but I like it. Let's take a walk."

Connie followed Regina from the room. They walked through the kitchen and into a staff hallway.

"Did you know that boy?"

"From the meeting? I knew he did coffee."

"Yeah, he worked with Sarah's husband."

"Are we okay?"

Regina unlocked a door. "—You're going home."

Connie's husband and daughters were waiting for her. She stood for a moment unsure— they looked older than she remembered, women now. It'd only been a couple of months but things had changed. She didn't know who to hug first. Bridget put her arms around her mother. Connie, in gratitude, broke. "—I'm so sorry, sweetheart. I love you so much."

"We missed you, mom."

Robert stood to the side as her daughters held her. When the hugs subsided, she smiled at Robert. She reached for his hand. He returned the touch, but Connie felt something less— she felt his distrust, a tentative welcome, and years of unrequited pain.

PREACHER

The Tuesday night meeting was podium participation. It was a light crowd, but they were well-organized, and there were newcomers and visitors from afar. There was a young thug in the far row— slicked-back hair, 'Vans' tattooed over his left eye. Albert summed him up— *That's one of my people. God put me here to minister to alcoholics like him— to give my testimony. If I'm called on, I know what to say— a message of 'depth and weight.'*

A few minutes before the break, Albert's name was called. He was ready. As he walked to the front of the room, his hopeful convert, the young thug walked outside with a vape in his hand.

"Good evening, I'm Beto Fernández, and I am an alcoholic."

They militantly returned his greeting.

"And if you're new, there's some things that you must be doing to stay here. I'd suggest you get a sponsor with time, but suggestion is a very weak word. You *must* get a sponsor with a working knowledge of our literature and you *must* stop playing your game. Any fool can come in here and run a mouth. Read your pages, 86 through 89— every day, and say those prayers. You *must* do these things if you want what we have!"

After the meeting, a few of the Tuesday-nighters shook his hand, clapped him on the back, and told him how far he'd come. He was charged.

Sometimes I think James leaves too much for chance. That 'people hear when they can hear' thing sounds like a cop-out to me. I wish somebody would've forced this stuff on me years ago— scared straight, that's what I needed, a strong message of recovery and a strong hand to guide me.

Still reeling from the high, Albert stopped at a service station. A lifted Chevelle pulled in front of him and backed up to the pump. Albert rolled his window down. "—Hey, *Vato*. I was going there."

The man in the Chevy shut off his car and got out. He was a big, white bro with tribal ink on his worked-out arms.

"Hey *Vato*— I said that's me."

The man inserted his credit card and paid Albert no mind. He popped open the hatch and removed the fuel cap.

Albert got out and approached him. "—Hey, can you hear me, man? That's my spot."

"Fuck you." The man inserted the nozzle and turned his back on Albert.

Oh, a sick man. Take a breath, Beto. You can't get bent out of shape every time some fucking puto *wants to act like a bitch. Your thinking is a defect of character. You need to do a third step on that and just let it go. Easy does it. One day at a time.*

Albert turned toward his car, and then he heard a voice.

"What up, Donnie?" Chevy Chevelle had a friend. The man opened the passenger door and stepped out.

"Fucking spic with a paint-job trying to get tough. Motherfucker's been watching too many Zapata movies."

The men laughed as Albert's pride-filled program descended to the oil-stained pavement. He disconnected— floating as if he were high, watching the world in slow motion. He kicked 'Donnie' face-first into the gas pump and then stomped on the back of his head— his open mouth kissing concrete, cracking teeth and bone. His partner moved quick, but Albert was quicker. Two swift jabs, a hook, and a well-placed uppercut sent the second bro lights-out to the ground. After a few well-placed stomps for good measure, Albert beat the men with the gas nozzle and sprayed them with a dose of ninety-three percent octane. He patted his pants pockets for a match as a chorus of honks and screams brought him back into reality.

What the fuck just happened, man? What did I do?

Dazed, he drifted back to his car, oblivious to the wave of chaos now breaking around him. He watched as his freshly bruised hand opened the door, his body climbed behind the steering wheel, and the old Albert adjusted the rearview and started the car.

He drove off, wondering what happened to the new Beto, thinking of Tina, and feeling as if he wasn't going to make it.

He was still on empty.

*****

"I don't understand. I asked you to drive me out to my father's grave— it's part of the program. I want to make amends."

"Your program, not mine, Connie. I've got things to do. You're gonna have to find another way out there."

"What the hell is with you guys? You've never denied me, Robert."

"You're right— I've lived like a god-damn dog at your heels for the last twenty-five years. I've had enough."

"What are you saying? You want a divorce?"

"I'm saying I'm not playing it your way anymore. The kids and I are tired of your shit. It was pretty nice around here with you gone."

There was a row of crystal figurines on the shelf— trinkets of trips gone by. Connie swept them to the floor— the memories shattering on polished hardwood. "I'm fucking sober! What the fuck do you want from me?"

Robert kept his cool. His gaze steady, unflinching. "—If that's what sober looks like, I prefer drunk."

He walked out of the room.

Connie stood shaking on the carpet— the adrenaline, the anger, the shock, the disbelief that her family could treat her like this now that she was walking a spiritual path.

You prefer drunk, I'll show you drunk, you fucking asshole.

There was a wooden cabinet in the corner— a mid-century, home liquor bar. She grabbed a bottle of Cognac aged forty years and a crystal snifter. Stepping over the broken figurines she took a seat in front of the fireplace, opened the bottle, and poured two fingers of the expensive gold libation. The light from the window sweeping through the glass turned the Cognac a sweet caramel brown.

It was a fucking joke, anyway. I didn't need rehab— they just wanted me out of their lives. That was their way of getting me gone.

She picked up the glass and inhaled the scent— instantly, as if from a hot flame— she recoiled.

I'm out of my fucking mind.

She threw the glass into the fireplace and grabbed her phone. She called Bayside.

"Hello, Bayside."

"I need to speak to Regina. It's an emergency."

"I can't give information out on clients."

"She's not a client, she's a case worker. This is Connie Phillips. I just got released from there. Please get her."

"One moment."

The elevator theme music played one note at a time— soft, graceful fragments of light, filled pastures of serenity, gliding endlessly into moments of tranquility and—*pick up the fucking phone!*

"Princess?"

"Help me— I think I need to come back."

"What's going on? Did you drink?"

"No, but I had it in my hand. I wanted to… my family… "

"What about your family?"

"Nobody cares if I'm sober. I've done everything I'm supposed to. My girls don't have time for me, and Robert isn't helping. I can't fucking stand this. Why can't they see it?"

"Oh, is the world being hard on you?"

"What?"

"I get it. You want credit for doing what normal people do every day. You want a medal for not killing yourself."

"No, it's not that. I just want them to see what a good job I'm doing. I want them to appreciate me!"

The tears of a sober life carved new pathways down Connie's cheeks.

"You're feeling sorry for yourself."

"I am not. This is real."

"Oh, I know, it's real. The one thing you can say about self-pity is it is sincere. Princess, it's life on life's terms, not life on Connie's. You inflicted years of damage on your family. You can't expect that to disappear in a few months. There's a long road of reparations in front of you and some of it is going to suck."

"Okay."

"What's the damage over there— anything other than your thoughts."

"Some broken glass— I yelled at Robert."

"Clean up the glass, keep your mouth shut, and when things calm down, apologize for your behavior. Try to see Robert's point of view— don't be a doormat, but understand it's gonna take time. Now, where are you with the program?"

"I was gonna go out to my dad's grave. I needed a ride— I gave up my license on that last case, and Robert said no."

"Good. I'm glad he's becoming his own man. I think in the long run you might find that attractive. Now, are you willing to seek other options regarding your father?"

"Yes."

"I'm gonna send you my friend's contact. Call her."

"What do I say?"

"Tell her what you told me."

"Okay, I'll do it. Thank you."

She disconnected the call and opened the contact— Sarah.

A BALCONY CHAT

James was watching the waves when his phone rang. He hadn't been in the water for years, but it was still in his heart.

"Hey Beto, what's happening?"

"I need to talk to you— it's important."

"Okay, when do you want to meet?"

"Can I come up?"

"You're here?"

"Yeah, I'm outside. I've been sitting here for a while."

"You're stalking me— do I need a restraining order?"

"Come on, man. This hurts."

"Come up."

Sarah let him in and walked him to the balcony— *I was going to tease Albert— make light, tell James his playdate was here, but I could see the pain in his eyes. I think some of these new guys think getting sober is a free ride— that once they're clean they're good. I hope he didn't drink.*

"Hey, boss." He hugged James— longer than a casual hello.

"You don't mind the smoke, do you?" James took his usual seat and lit a cigar.

"No. I tell you right now it's the best thing I need. Thank you for seeing me."

"What's going on, buddy— hold up, did you drink?"

"No."

"Pills, weed, mood-altering, mind-changing?"

"No. Fuck no."

"Okay, then. Let's relax and hash it out— hit it."

"I'm not sure where to start. I think I owe you an apology."

"For what?"

"For thinking this is easier than it is. I was full of spiritual pride— telling people what they need to do. I thought I was healed— how the fuck do you keep that ego in check? I was up at the podium talking 'depth and weight—'"

"What the fuck? Where did you get that?"

"It's in the book."

"I know it's in the book, but it's a passage that's often abused. When you hear guys talking like that, they're usually getting ready to recite lines verbatim— things they've heard people say that they have no real experience with. We drop from the heart here, not from the head."

"Okay, I get it."

"And one more thing— how much depth and weight is in a kind word, a welcome, a cup of coffee and a handshake— god-damn it, Beto. The last thing we need is another fucking pulpit thumper around here."

"I hear you."

"What else?"

"I got in a fight."

"Oh, how the mighty have fallen."

"I had no control— one minute I'm hand in hand with Jesus and the next I'm beating on some fool."

"That's how it works— the higher you roll, the harder you'll fall."

"How do you do it? People come up to you all the time, quoting you in meetings, asking for help— how do you stay so small?"

"Self-flagellation."

"What?"

"I'm fucking with you."

James re-lit his cigar and smiled at his young friend.

"Albert, I know I'm not immune. I've seen guys with a hell of a lot more time than I have go out. I also don't play God. I can't see the future and I'm unsure about my past so how would I know what's best for you? I'm a servant, Beto, not a master. Somewhere down the line, these guys got it screwed up. They think being called a sponsor puts them on top, but the highest you can get around here— and this knowledge will always keep you right-sized, is that we are here to serve— servant not master. Remember that."

"Okay."

"It sounds to me like *you* were playing God. Are you ready to bring Him out of retirement?"

"Yes."

"Another in a long succession of surrenders… and what else is on your mind— the *real* issue?"

"How the fuck do you know there's something else?"

"I got the all-seeing eye tattooed on my chest. Spill it."

"I felt like shit after the fight. I knew a drink wouldn't help, but I was really uncomfortable. I called Tina, and I slept with her."

"Okay."

"That's it, no advice?"

"I try not to give advice and your sex life is none of my business. However, if you want my opinion… "

"Here it comes."

"Do you want to be with her, or are you just using her to feel better?"

"It was mutual."

"It's never mutual. I don't care if she agrees to it or not. If you're selfishly using someone, it speaks to your character. It says that there's been no psychic change and you'll probably end up drunk."

"Can we go back to where you don't give advice?"

"Beto, the most pain I was ever in was sober. It was wrapped around cheating and lying and trying to make myself feel better by sleeping around. It doesn't work."

"I understand."

"When you leave here today, maybe take a minute to speak with your God. Ask that those defects be taken away— ask that you're filled with kindness and understanding. You'll be alright, God has your back."

THE VOICE BENEATH

James was in his office working on a story for a local paper when Sarah interrupted his flow.

"Hey baby, sorry to bug, but can you do me the biggest favor in the world?"

"I'm not sitting down to pee. I believe a man's gotta right to splash a little piss about if he feels so inclined."

"A woman from Bayside called."

"Yeah, what's up with her?"

"Regina gave her my number— thought maybe you could help. She wants to make amends to her father, and she needs a ride. Will you do it?"

"Yeah, sure, but why the *big favor*?"

"He's buried on the peninsula about ninety miles from here— you could ask Albert to ride along."

"I think there's a casino out there, " He pulled out his phone. "let me check my funds and I'll give you the definitive."

"God-damn it, James. You know there's a casino, and the last time we were up there, you got your ass kicked. Remember, you told me to hold the bank cards and not give them back no matter what— ten minutes later you were pounding on the car window threatening to call the police because I "stole" your ATM card. I recall leaving your jonesing ass at the bus station."

"Was that up there?"

"You know it was. How about you practice a little slot machine abstinence while you're doing this— serve her, not the shiny metal monkey on your back. Albert doesn't need to be drug into that crap."

*****

James and Connie were in the front seats. Albert was in the back. The vanity mirror was down and Connie carefully touched up her lipstick— "Regina told me to ask you about a blank page. She said it was your favorite— is that true?"

"You never told me about a blank page, James."

"I didn't have to; you were already clueless."

He focused on the road, the gas steadily applied, the brakes lightly touched.

"The first page in our book of recovery is blank, and it's the hardest page to follow." James paused for a moment and gathered his words. "The blank page represents an open mind— untouched. We come here full of preconceived notions about God, about ourselves, about alcoholism, and the hardest thing to do is unlearn what we think we know— especially with a Higher Power."

James moved to the right and let a faster car pass.

"Is that why you don't talk about your God?"

"I don't?"

"You told me not to tell anyone you prayed. Did you think I forgot?"

"I don't think you forget anything. I don't pray... if necessary, I chat. My conception of God has changed. When I came here, I had the God of my grandmother, but I cut Him loose."

Connie reapplied her lipstick— "But you believe in God, right?"

"You tell me you believe in God, so what... even *demons* believe in God."

"Is that in the blue book?"

"No. It's from the Book of James. Show me you believe in God by the way you treat others. Did you know some folks wanted to call what we do the James Gang?" He moved into the slow lane and let another car pass. "Beto says I never talk about God, but I do. When I talk about spirit, about love, intelligence, and heart, I'm talking about God. When I stick my hand out to a newcomer, when I kiss my wife. I'm always talking about God, and I listen for that soft, small voice inside. *Sotto voce...*"

They came upon a slow vehicle. James didn't pass.

"What does that mean? Italian? I do a wicked chicken parm. You guys should come by."

James slowed down— cruised three ticks below the speed limit.

"There's a term in music— *sotto voce*, it means the soft voice beneath." A car rocketed past James, narrowly missing an oncoming car. Albert was antsy.

"Look at Beto. He can't stand me driving behind this motherfucker. How long has your dad been dead, Connie?"

"Twelve years."

"Twelve years dead, and Beto's in a fucking hurry to get over there. I used to be like that, always in a hurry. Trying to get my hands on everything— squeezing the world so fucking tight. No wonder I had to drink."

"I don't feel thirsty."

"Not now you don't, but if I took it any slower you'd start salivating."

"Shit, I know what's coming now. Another life lesson from the King of the Kitchen. Listen up, Connie. This man has a story for any occasion— some of them true."

"Fine, I'll keep it to myself. Go fuck yourself, Beto."

"No, come on. I'm fucking with you James. You were the one who told me I needed to lighten up— I'm practicing."

"Ha! You need to practice listening... anyway, as I was about to say," he winked at Albert. "I'd come up on a car like this, and the fucking orchestra in my head would go wild.

"I'd pull up on his bumper— real close, and the kettledrums would pound in my head— kill him, kill him, kill him! And then the horns would scream to life— pull alongside and flip him off, pull alongside and flip him off! And then those strings, those big, beautiful strings, would take control and with all power they'd sing— get in front and slow down, get in front and slow down. Now this poor fucker hasn't done a fucking thing— except the speed limit, and me and that orchestra are running wild until... *sotto voce*... the small voice beneath slowly rises, and do you know what it says? It says, let it go... just let it go. And sometimes I do."

THE GRAVEYARD

The graveyard was on a point overlooking the bay. They parked by the gates and walked down a poorly-tended dirt path. Connie's father was resting beneath a moss-stained marble stone under a wind-swept coastal pine.

"What should I do?"

"When I made amends to my father, I sat at his grave and I shared my life. I told him where I'd been, and where I was now. Were you on good terms with your pops?"

"No. I quit speaking to him when I realized he never listened. I didn't have a voice."

"How do you feel about making amends?"

"I wronged him, and to successfully complete the steps, I need to right my wrongs."

"I didn't ask Bayside what they felt. I'm asking you. You're not angry?"

"I am, but we keep that to ourselves."

"He's dead, Connie. Maybe you have some things you need to say before you clean it up."

"Can we do that?"

"I wouldn't suggest it if he were alive, but this might be a good time to reclaim your power. Pray first, ask for a clear channel, and then unload your burden. Let him know how you felt and how he let you down. Yell if you need to, scream and cry and curse him as if he was on his knees before you, and then, when you're done, clean your side of the street— see where you were wrong, and shoulder your part. Take your time. Beto and I are gonna wander around, see what kind of trouble we can get into. Go ahead, Connie— he can't hurt you now."

She took off her sweater and used it as a blanket to cover the bare earth. A dialogue began that climbed in volume with every word.

The boys went their separate ways— a path along the cliff's edge for Albert, and James threaded his way between the graves.

As the coffee maker walked, he thought of the man that brought him the message. He was still alive, still sober. He thought of his father— dead. His first wife— dead. The many alcoholics that had for a time joined him on this path— now dead. He thought of Jacob and his family— the years of pain to come, their first Christmas without him, a birthday, a graduation, a wedding, and maybe even grandchildren. They would miss him at every turn.

The grass was wet beneath his feet, and with each step he took, he sank deeper into a morass of self-pity.

Fuck, I'm getting old. When I came into the program, I was young and my body didn't hurt in the morning and when I pissed I could knock toilet paper off the side of the bowl. When I got sober, I could still see without glasses and my hair was growing where it ought to and most of my teeth were still chattering away in my mouth. I could go all night when I got here, and now I'm stoked if I can go at all.

He wondered if the outcome was worth it and without thinking, he stepped onto a grave. It was the author Raymond Carver. He read the inscription on the stone:

GRAVY

"No other word will do. For that's what it was. Gravy. Gravy, these past ten years. Alive, sober, working, loving, and being loved by a good woman. Eleven years ago he was told he had six months to live at the rate he was going. And he was going nowhere but down. So he changed his ways somehow. He quit drinking! And the rest? After that it was all gravy, every minute of it, up to and including when he was told about, well, some things that were breaking down and building up inside his head. "Don't weep for me," he said to his friends. "I'm a lucky man. I've had ten years longer than I or anyone expected. Pure Gravy. And don't forget it."

Fucking-a, man. This cat had ten years, and I have thirty. Thirty years of walking on the sunny side of the street— eating off plates, sleeping indoors. I couldn't have asked for better, and if it was all taken away— if today was my last, I could say the same— pure gravy.

About the Author

James T. is a sober member in good standing of various twelve-step groups. He lives in Northern California with his wife Sarah and their two cats: William and Robert. He is an avid collector of automatons and religious artifacts. His favorite quote is: "What's wrong with you?"

Printed in Great Britain
by Amazon

47321996R00121